"I'm used to it."

The Saint Disciple took off her black-rimmed glasses. Lord Mask wasn't just imagining that her eyes seemed even sharper now that she'd removed her thin frames.

"I mean, this is the *fourth time* I've been twenty-two."

Risya In Empire

Adviser of Lord Yunmelngen. Saint Disciple of the fifth seat. Former classmate of Mismis's and a woman of innumerable gifts. Faces up against Lord Mask, the adviser of the Zoa, at the Queen's Palace.

7

KEI SAZANE

Illustration by
Ao Nekonabe

NEW YORK

Our Last CRUSADE OR THE RISE OF A New World

7 KEI SAZANE

Translation by Jan Cash
Cover art by Ao Nekonabe

This book is a work of fiction. Names, characters, places, and incidents are the product of the author's imagination or are used fictitiously. Any resemblance to actual events, locales, or persons, living or dead, is coincidental.

KIMI TO BOKU NO SAIGO NO SENJO, ARUIWA SEKAI GA HAJIMARU SEISEN Vol.7
©Kei Sazane, Ao Nekonabe 2019
First published in Japan in 2019 by KADOKAWA CORPORATION, Tokyo.
English translation rights arranged with KADOKAWA CORPORATION, Tokyo, through TUTTLE-MORI AGENCY, INC., Tokyo.

English translation © 2021 by Yen Press, LLC

Yen Press, LLC supports the right to free expression and the value of copyright. The purpose of copyright is to encourage writers and artists to produce the creative works that enrich our culture.

The scanning, uploading, and distribution of this book without permission is a theft of the author's intellectual property. If you would like permission to use material from the book (other than for review purposes), please contact the publisher. Thank you for your support of the author's rights.

Yen On
150 West 30th Street, 19th Floor
New York, NY 10001

Visit us at yenpress.com
facebook.com/yenpress
twitter.com/yenpress
yenpress.tumblr.com
instagram.com/yenpress

First Yen On Edition: October 2021

Yen On is an imprint of Yen Press, LLC.
The Yen On name and logo are trademarks of Yen Press, LLC.

The publisher is not responsible for websites (or their content) that are not owned by the publisher.

Cataloging in Publication data is on file with the Library of Congress.

ISBNs: 978-1-9753-2210-6 (paperback)
978-1-9753-2211-3 (ebook)

10 9 8 7 6 5 4 3 2 1

LSC-C

Printed in the United States of America

Our Last Crusade
OR THE RISE OF A
New World

deus So Ee suo Sez et heckt Eeo?
Do you all believe that I have denied you?

van Eez d-kfen uc phanisis getie.
You're just afraid to face your own weakness.

Shie-la So xedelis. Sew olfey tis-lisya-Ye-harp.
Remember that I nurtured you by loving you always.

LOU FAMILY VILLA: LOU ERZ MANSION

Second Floor (In flight from assassins sent by the Hydra)

Mismis Klass

The commander of Unit 907. Baby-faced and often mistaken for a child, but actually a legal adult. Klutzy but responsible. Trusts her subordinates. Became a witch after plunging into a vortex.

Jhin Syulargun

The sniper of Unit 907. Prides himself on his deadly aim. Can't seem to shake off Iska, since they trained under the same mentor. Cool and sarcastic, though he has a soft spot for his buddies.

Nene Alkastone

Chief mechanic of Unit 907. Weapon-making genius. Mastered operation of a satellite that releases armor-piercing shots from a high altitude. Thinks of Iska as her older brother. Wide-eyed and loveable.

Sisbell Lou Nebulis IX

Youngest princess of Nebulis. Aliceliese's little sister. Saved by Iska one year prior when she was captured in the Empire. Possesses Illumination, which reproduces footage of past events and makes her a target of the Hydra.

FIRST FLOOR (IN BATTLE)

Iska

Successor of the Black Steel. Member of Special Defense Third Division, Unit 907. Used to be a part of the highest rank in the military, the Saint Disciples. Stripped of his title for helping a witch (Sisbell) break out of prison. Currently fighting Talisman to prevent him from kidnapping Sisbell.

Talisman

Head of the three royal families (the Hydra). Orchestrator of the plot to kill the queen. Hides his aggressive true personality behind a neutral mask and demeanor. Attacks the vacation home to abduct Sisbell.

STAR SPIRE

PALACE OF NEBULIS

Elletear Lou Nebulis IX
Princess of Nebulis. Eldest daughter of the Lou. Known for having very weak astral powers.

QUEEN'S PALACE

— QUEEN'S PALACE —

Nebulis IIX
The queen. Mother to three daughters. Seems to have history with Salinger, the transcendental sorcerer…

Joheim
The "Flash" Knight. Saint Disciple of the first seat.

MOON SPIRE

— MIDAIR CORRIDOR —

Kissing
The golden child of the Zoa. Purebred of thorns.

Mei
The "Incessant Tempest." Saint Disciple of the third seat.

— MIDAIR GARDEN —

Growley
Head of one of the three royal bloodlines (the Zoa).

Nameless
The Invisible Hand of God. Saint Disciple of the eighth seat.

On
Lord Mask. Head of family by proxy.

Risya In Empire
Adviser of the Lord. Saint Disciple of the fifth seat.

SUN SPIRE

— EN ROUTE TO THE ROYAL PALACE FROM THE VILLA —

Aliceliese Lou Nebulis IX
Second-born princess of Nebulis. Strongest astral mage, who attacks with ice. Feared by the Empire as the Ice Calamity Witch. Rivals with Iska, an enemy swordsman she met on the battlefield.

Rin Vispose
Alice's attendant. An astral mage controlling earth. Maid uniform conceals weapons for assassination. Skilled at deadly espionage. Has an inferiority complex about her chest.

(Not yet infiltrated by Saint Disciples)

Our Last CRUSADE OR THE RISE OF A New World

CONTENTS

Prologue	001	Lord Yunmelngen
Chapter 1	007	Night of the Witch Hunt, Part I
Chapter 2	029	Night of the Witch Hunt, Part II
Chapter 3	067	Night of the Witch Hunt, Part III
Chapter 4	097	The Unforgiven
Chapter 5	103	Aliceliese the Ice Calamity Witch
Intermission	119	Our Last Battle or the Night of Shed Tears
Chapter 6	129	Our Twisted Battle or the Night of Promised Vows
Epilogue 1	153	Darkest Before Dawn
Epilogue 2	159	A Girl Offering Prayers to Ten Billion Stars
Afterword	163	

PROLOGUE

Lord Yunmelngen

The Heavenly Empire—a territory united and built like a fortress.

All political decisions were made here in the Imperial country, which controlled the largest mass of land in the world. Legislature was handled by the Imperial Senate, and military objectives were issued by army headquarters and executed only upon receiving approval from the Lord.

On the topmost floor of the oldest tower in the Imperial capital—the Heaven Between Insight and Nosight…

"I have a report for you, Your Excellency. We've launched our attack on the palace in Nebulis."

"……"

"Of course, this *is* their palace—said to be the Planetary Stronghold. The forces that are invading are elite but few. I imagine they'll face some difficulty conquering the place."

The messenger was a burly, mustached man in a military uniform. No one in this nation was oblivious to his identity.

It was the Lord Yunmelngen himself—or so the public were led to believe.

"It's been almost thirty minutes post-invasion," continued the man.

"...*And?*"

"By flames and by night, four Saint Disciples have successfully infiltrated the palace."

This austere man with a mustache could be seen at all Imperial ceremonies as the Lord. The truth was...he was just a body double for the real Lord behind the thin curtain.

"The three Saint Disciples—Risya, Mei, and Nameless—have each located the Founder's descendants. They have started to engage in battle, working to eliminate the threats."

"*And Joheim?*"

"He's acting alone, on his way to the Queen's Space. It's been fifteen minutes since our last communication with him. He might have already fallen to the hands of the enemy."

"*...Or he's locked in combat with the queen,*" rasped an aged, hoarse voice from beyond the curtain. It sounded like someone on their sickbed, just barely holding on, nearing their final breath. "*Nuisances, those Eight Great Apostles.*"

Behind the curtain, the Lord's shadow quivered as if backlit by candlelight. A soft sigh was audible enough to be heard.

"*I understand the plan was to attack the palace while the Founder Nebulis slumbers—to capture the purebreds. I imagine the Founder will not be happy with me once she's awake.*"

"I would imagine."

"*I would like that* thing *to continue slumbering for a while.*" Another sigh from behind the curtain.

That concluded the report. The two secretaries serving the body double bowed and left the room. Only the middle-aged man—the double himself—remained in the Lord's presence.

A hush fell over them. The Heaven Between Insight and No-sight was dead silent.

PROLOGUE

"If I may, Your Excellency." The body double cleared his throat. "If you would humor me with some small talk: Did you recently slip out into the business district in the capital?"

The body double kept his eyes fixed on the other side of the curtain, staring hard at the silhouette.

"According to rumors on First Avenue, the military police officers received a report from a young woman claiming she saw a strange beast—a silver fox walking on two legs."

"..."

"I believe I requested you to refrain from reckless excursions?"

"Hmm...? I don't remember anyone saying that about me." The voice behind the curtain was almost unrecognizable. It sounded almost lively now, as if someone was holding back laughter, like a boy soprano. *"But I suppose your memory is better than mine."*

The curtain swished open...

...It revealed a humanoid, silver beast who chuckled softly.

The figure sat on woven tatami mats, bipedal fox legs crossed. Its fingers were articulated like a human hand. The silhouette wasn't entirely animalistic—only the body was fox-like, while the face was nearly human. In other words, a therianthrope, like something straight out of a fairy tale. The monster cackled in delight.

"..." The body double said nothing. After all, this silvery beast was his master.

"Ha-ha, that reminds me." The leader of the largest military state in the world, *Lord Yunmelngen*, sounded elated. *"Has it already been thirty years? I think I remember seeing a young boy scampering away in tears after seeing poor old Meln."*

"I remember shrinking in terror like it was yesterday." The

body double nodded. "I daresay the girl who witnessed you must have had a similar fright."

"It's all written in the stars. That child from thirty years ago is now my double. You're certainly playing the part, growing your facial hair and talking to me. Not a bad life now, is it?"

"..."

"Maybe I'll make that girl my tenth double. Give it another ten years." A bushy tail swished as the Lord looked up into empty space, seemingly entertained.

The Founder Nebulis revolted only a century ago...a relatively short period of time compared to the history behind the title of Lord. The person to receive this title was chosen through a clandestine method called the Ascension Ceremony, which was kept secret even from the Imperial citizens. Below the surface and hidden from history, the only ones changing office were the body doubles.

The leader of the Empire had never changed. The one with the self-anointed nickname of Meln reigned over the Empire.

"I bet I sound like a broken record at this point, but..." The silvery beast stretched a humanlike hand out into the air, its connected arm covered in fur like a fox or a wolf. *"The astral energy bubbling from the core of this planet is extremely strong. It can push life to new levels."*

"I take it that you're referring to your own body?"

"Hmm? I'm not talking about myself right now." The Lord's mouth formed a grin—sharp, wolfish canines peeking from the sides. *"Apparently, another witch has been born in the Nebulis Sovereignty. And I'm not talking about the Founder. That's why I went out of my way to dispatch Risya—so she can investigate. And I did drop the tiniest hint to the transcendental sorcerer."*

"Do you mean Test Subject E?"

PROLOGUE

"I imagine this new witch will reveal itself during our raid. Anyway, enough about that..." The silvery beast looked up at the ceiling, contemplating something. *"...This certainly places us in a bind. The Empire is currently attacking the palace. If the Founder wakes, she'll take her anger out on me. Well, I suppose I didn't do enough to stop the Eight Great Apostles. I didn't want to get caught up in their mess."*

The Lord shrugged, like there were no other options. These gestures were remarkably human.

"Founder Nebulis." Now, the fox-like figure sounded intimidating, as if the ferocious beast inside was seeping out. *"It seems your country will transform as you slumber from a dream you can't wake from. But this wasn't the Empire's bidding. Your own descendants sought out this war."*

CHAPTER 1

Night of the Witch Hunt, Part I

1

The Nebulis palace.

Home to the Founder's descendants, it prided itself on an impregnable defense that the Imperial forces had failed to get past.

The Planetary Stronghold was constructed by crystallized astral power that had been summoned by ancient techniques. Nestled by the jet-black night sky, it towered over the earth like a luminous coral reef.

The castle was up in flames.

Billowing under the wind, embers settled on the lawn and set it ablaze. The flames lapping at the outer walls of the castle were only getting stronger, showing no signs of dying down any time soon.

"Rin! Hurry!"

And now…Moon Diadem, the suspended corridor connecting

the palace towers, exploded as Alice looked on from the window of Cadillac One.

"...How can this be happening?"

Hundreds of tons of rubble came crashing down from the sky. If there had been astral corps in its trajectory, the casualties sustained would have been incalculable.

"Please don't worry, Lady Alice. We knew that would happen," Rin answered, gripping the steering wheel from her position in the driver's seat. "The midair corridor was designed to detach from other towers, a mechanism to prevent anyone from reaching the Queen's Palace in the event of an Imperial raid. The castle's defenses are working properly. This is *good* news."

"......"

But, Rin, isn't that the same as a lizard severing its tail to use as a decoy? Alice mentally questioned. It was sacrifice for survival's sake. Wasn't this the same thing as signaling to the Imperial forces that they had the mages cornered?

"These flames are the real problem. Could the Imperial troops have opened fire on the fuel tanks tucked away...?" Rin gritted her back teeth.

Crack. At that moment, a small hole bored through the windshield of Cadillac One.

Was it a sniper? If they were shooting this car using specialized bullets, that had to mean...

"Rin, get out!"

Alice opened the door of the back seat, flinging herself out of the vehicle. Rin evacuated the driver's seat. As they rolled across the dark lawn, a firebomb hit the car, which instantly burst into flames.

"I knew it. They're taking cover in the night to shoot at us!"

CHAPTER 1

"Lady Alice, I'll go first. We don't know how many Imperial soldiers are on the grounds! Please watch out for stray bullets!"

As hellfire crackled all around them, Rin sprinted farther into the premises. Alice followed, heading to the Queen's Palace—the tower housing her mother, Queen Nebulis IIX.

"Lady Alice! You're alive!" Members of the astral corps turned to look at her.

Illuminated by the raging flames, Alice's royal dress—pure white in color—was so beautiful that they momentarily forgot it was her battle uniform. It also screamed her presence. Uniquely crafted for direct descendants of Nebulis, this outfit had been made so her subjects could recognize her at a glance.

"Fill me in on the situation," Alice ordered.

"Yes, ma'am! We've been concentrating on protecting the Queen's Palace. We've helped all civilians evacuate the towers into the underground shelters."

"Any attacks on the bunkers?"

"None to note. The stationed astral corps are guarding them. Based on reports, the mercenaries from the Hydra have come to serve as reinforcements."

"…I'll make sure to thank Lord Talisman."

That left two other concerns: guaranteeing the queen's safety and containing the spreading fire. Left unattended, the flames could cause injury outside the palace grounds.

"Please hurry to Her Majesty, the queen!" Several astral corps members ran toward her, out of breath. "We'll take care of—"

"Stop!" Alice screamed.

Exploding beside them was a mass of fire—too large to view its full magnitude. It engulfed the astral corps. Alice's powers had automatically activated as soon as she sensed the explosion. All she could manage was a wall made from a thin film of ice, only a fraction of an inch thick.

"Uh... Ack!"

"Are you all—?!"

Blowing through the ice wall, the wind blasted across the astral corps. Even their heat-resistant uniforms could not absorb the impact. Alice didn't act fast enough to cover for them. Her subordinates collapsed to the ground, their backs badly burned.

"Lady Alice, are you all right?!" Rin asked.

"Don't worry about me! Worry about these four... We need medics! Where are the medics?! Over here!" Alice shouted.

She knew the brutal truth, however. *Medics were never going to come.* Collapsed all over the palace grounds were members of the astral corps.

"Rin! Create a golem. Take these four to the underground shelter in the House of Lou. Doctors should be on standby there. I'll wait here."

"Wh-what?! But, Lady Alice—," Rin stammered.

Their objective was to head to the Queen's Palace. That would require leaving the collapsed soldiers.

"I'm thinking clearly... I'm trying to, at least." Alice ground her teeth, slowly shaking her head. "My mother has her own guards. The Queen's Palace has perfect defenses, so the worst casualties will be on the palace grounds."

"..."

"Come back within fifteen minutes. In the meantime, I'll work on extinguishing the flames."

"As you wish." Rin bowed. The ground behind her rose, bringing life to a gigantic golem that cradled the wounded soldiers. "I intend to come back in precisely fifteen minutes, but I expect there

CHAPTER 1

to be Imperial soldiers in my path. If I'm late by even a minute, please head to the Queen's Palace, Lady Alice."

Rin and her golem ran into the night, embers trailing after them.

Fifteen minutes.

That should be fine, Alice told herself as she breathed out.

…It'll be fine. I know this is the right choice.

…Even a Saint Disciple won't be able to get all the way into the Queen's Palace in this span.

Not even Iska. Not even Nameless. Alice knew that Saint Disciples were elite soldiers to be feared, but the palace was a living labyrinth created by astral powers. Without knowing how the tower was constructed, it was impossible to reach the Queen's Space.

"Astral corps, listen closely!" Alice strained her voice, trying to talk over the crackling inferno. "I'll contain the fire here using my astral power. Things are going to get dangerous. Retreat behind me immediately!"

She would remain on the grounds and prioritize extinguishing the flames.

…At this time, Alice didn't know that she would come to regret that choice.

2

Nebulis Sovereignty. Central state.

The countryside was quaint and woodsy. Outside the city, snowy vales stretched toward the distant horizon. This area housed a villa owned by Queen Nebulis IIX from the House of Lou. The Lou Erz mansion.

The ivory castle stood on a plot of land that stretched as far as the eye could see. No renovations had been made to its exterior, but the automatic door equipped with surveillance devices was just one of many state-of-the-art technologies that had replaced the interior of the building.

The castle had started to crumble.

The ceiling of the main hall on the first floor had caved in, its four walls pockmarked with holes. The second floor was in an even worse state. Intermittent gunfire echoed down the corridors.

"They found us *again*...! Boss! Nene! This way!" yelled Jhin, the silver-haired sniper, in between gunshots at the two members from Unit 907. He was clutching the hand of the girl who huddled close to his side.

"Eeeek!"

"We're getting out of here. Where's our next hiding spot?"

"I-in the back!" Holding his hand, Sisbell started to scramble forward.

A girl with big doe eyes and glossy strawberry-blond hair. She looked cute with the faint glow on her cheeks and lips, though she seemed visibly nervous.

She must have been fourteen—maybe fifteen. He didn't know her actual age. As an Imperial soldier, Jhin had no use for that information. He'd just been tasked to protect her. Plus, she was a witch. Had this been a battlefield, he would have turned his gun on her...

This was an exception. They had made a trade—guarding her in return for something that benefited them.

"We agreed to take her to the palace in exchange for getting those self-adhesives to hide astral crests for the boss... I knew it would be risky but not life-threateningly risky."

CHAPTER 1

"D-did you say something?!"

"Nothin'. You keep your head down and run. You get hit with one of those stray bullets, and you'll be in more pain than you thought possible," Jhin said as Sisbell ran beside him.

Their enemies were the astral corps from the Hydra, who were disguised as Imperial soldiers. Secretly organizing a coup against the queen, the Hydra had tried to silence Sisbell before she could reveal the truth using Illumination.

The assailants had attacked the residence, which landed Unit 907 in their current predicament.

"Hey! Can't you do something using your astral power? Like blast them away or whatever?"

"I wouldn't have hired guards if I could!"

"Then what about the servants?"

"The chefs and gardeners can't really fight. The servants might be able to defend themselves. If they don't hide, we'll have more casualties!" Sisbell practically yelled back.

They were obviously at a disadvantage in terms of firepower. The enemies pursuing them down the hallway were astral mages equipped with gear for Imperial troops. On the other hand, Jhin and the others were only carrying enough weapons for self-defense.

"D-don't you have a gun?!"

"It's for sniping. I haven't got the time to set it up for a melee in a mansion. Besides, I don't have enough ammo. I won't be able to take out all of them."

If he were going to train his scope on anyone, it'd be the enemy leader. In other words, he would have needed to snipe Talisman, the head of household, but Iska was holding that man back on the first floor. Right now, Jhin needed to focus on the safety of his ward, Sisbell.

"I guess we're going to be playing tag for a while."

"Oh...i-if we're just running, my astral power might be able to buy us some time."

"Really?"

"Only once. It's a bluff, so there will be no second chances." Sisbell put her hand to her chest and swung around to face behind, turning to the assailants after them. "—Planet, please show me your past."

The crest on her chest glowed with astral energy, its light manifesting an elaborate three-dimensional illusion that blocked the assassins. The mirage had produced an Imperial unit with over a dozen soldiers.

"What?!" The assassins immediately switched into a battle stance. Instantly, they registered the possibility that Imperial soldiers other than Unit 907 had been lurking in the mansion.

They failed to realize these troops were *their own disguised selves*.

"Tsk! I thought the report only mentioned four Imperial soldiers..."

"So there were more in hiding!"

They opened fire. The spray of bullets passed through the hologram. Right as the assassins realized this was Sisbell's doing, Jhin and the others ducked into the shadows of the stairs.

"Hey, boss! How are they looking?"

"I—I think we're fine. They've lost track of us...!" Commander Mismis listened for the sound of footsteps.

Next to her, Sisbell sat on the floor, panting. "Haah... Haah... Wh-what do you think? I tricked them."

"Can your astral power create hallucinations, too?"

"That was no hallucination. I just reproduced their raid,

CHAPTER 1

which occurred in this residence just a few minutes ago." Sisbell wiped away beads of sweat. "No one from the Sovereignty could keep their composure if armed Imperial soldiers appeared before them—in gear from the Empire, no less. That must have temporarily startled them."

"I see. That explains why you can't use that trick twice. They wouldn't fall for it a second time." Jhin glared at the landing of the stairs. They were on the second floor of the old castle. The head of the Hydra was on the first floor, stymied by Iska. Sisbell's room was on the third floor, but assassins would be waiting for her there.

"If we don't get out of here, we're going to be surrounded. You got any ideas for places we could jump out from on the second floor?"

"Uh… Wa…wa…ait."

"Oh. Yeah, don't talk. We'll buy time here until they find us."

She was in a state of shock. They'd been chased at gunpoint, after all. On top of that, this was her *vacation* home, and her enemy was another member of the royal family. She was taking things well, all things considered.

"But you'll never catch me praising a witch."

"What?"

"Nothing. Just keep quiet and listen to me. Shake your head when you want to say no."

"—"

"Let me confirm the situation. You're their target—that's obvious. Your pursuers are the House of Hydra, who are critical of the queen's bloodline. You're being pursued for your astral power, right?"

Illumination could reproduce the past in three dimensions,

which meant Sisbell could expose heinous crimes by re-creating the scene. Her power was ideal for analyzing information and gathering proof of wrongdoings.

That was why she was their target. She was being hunted by the masterminds behind the plot to assassinate the queen.

"And the name of the sketchy guy engaging with Iska is... Talisman, right? He's basically acknowledged that he's the one behind the whole thing."

"Lord Talisman?! Was it really you...?!"
"This was necessary. We require the Empire's power to reach the planet's core."

The head of the Hydra, Talisman. The man responsible for attacking this mansion had taken Jhin's interrogation with a smile. Had his collusion with the Empire been exposed, he wouldn't have just been labeled a traitor; he would have certainly been kicked out of the family. There must have been a reason why he had seemed so unperturbed.

"The success of his scheme relies on one thing: getting you out of the picture to obstruct the truth about the assassination from coming to the forefront. He needs to convince the people that Imperial soldiers were responsible for attacking this mansion and kidnapping you. And no one would doubt him; after all, *actual* Imperial forces are *raiding the royal palace* as we speak."

That was right. An attack orchestrated by the Hydra had commenced on the palace, which was located far from this villa.

"And there's another person in this picture: your sister Elletear. We only have circumstantial evidence regarding her involvement, so we'll try to prove that later. Either way, she's not in the mansion at the moment."

CHAPTER 1

"…Right."

"I'm going to say this just to be clear: We're Imperial subjects. It's completely normal for us to attack an enemy country—we've been at war for a hundred years, after all—so we don't give a damn what happens to your palace."

"…I understand."

"But we'll protect you," he told the girl whose large eyes darted around, uneasy.

Silently, Jhin motioned at her to get on her feet.

"I don't care if our soldiers are attacking or if you're an enemy witch. We're escorting you to the palace, so stop looking so mopey."

"Wh-who do you think you're calling mopey?!" Sisbell snapped, standing up. "A-and you're rude yourself!"

"If you have enough brainpower to talk back, you need to get your head into gear. The most important thing is getting out of here. I'm not picky. So tell me: Which second-floor window can we jump out of?"

The net was slowly closing in around them. Their only way of escape was outside. They wouldn't draw attention to themselves if they jumped into the gardens under the veil of night. If they made it to the city, the assassins wouldn't be able to catch them.

"They're dressed like Imperial soldiers, so if they take to the streets, they'll be mistaken for the enemy, and the astral corps will be out to get them. They aren't going to come after us."

"But what will we do about Iska?!"

"He'll figure it out."

"…But he's up against the royal family—and a head of household, at that."

"I won't deny that purebreds don't spell danger, but Iska won't have any problems. He'll be in trouble if he's hopelessly outnumbered, but he'll know when to get out of the situation before

CHAPTER 1

things start to look bad for him. Now keep quiet for a while." Jhin pressed a hand over Sisbell's mouth and looked at the commander next to him. "Boss, what's up with our pursuers?"

"Uh. I can't hear their footsteps. They might already be outside, thinking we got out of the mansion."

"This probably isn't the case, but I hope they split so some of them can keep guard outside... Hey."

"I—I hear you. You want me to lead the way, right?!" Sisbell nodded and pointed at the corridor. "Around the corner up ahead. There are several unused rooms and a dense thicket of trees outside the window, so I think it should be difficult for them to spot us."

Then she started walking.

As soon as her dainty feet began to move, the floor quietly creaked and sunk beneath her.

"...Huh?" Sisbell stopped in her tracks, sensing something was very wrong.

Her feet hadn't tread over the wine-colored carpet. In its place, she found a layer of crystallized white snow.

I've found you, Imperial soldiers—and Lady Sisbell.

"Sisbell, watch out!" Nene yanked her hand from behind.

The ceiling exploded, opening up to the third floor. Snow came pouring down like a waterfall.

"A blizzard inside the mansion? It's gotta be that old woman!" Jhin got his sniper rifle ready. He fired at the red witch he could make out from behind the snowy powder streaming from the ceiling.

"It's no use, Imperial soldier." The old woman was sucked into the snowstorm. "A cubic yard of packed snow can weigh half a ton.

It can absorb any sound, cushion any impact. Even a machine gun couldn't pierce through it, let alone such a puny little bullet."

The hallway in the Lou Erz mansion was flooded white, turning into a wintry landscape.

"You might have run away from me before, but it seems you cannot run for long—not with Miss Sisbell with you."

"'Sup, Grandma," Jhin snarled. "You're here."

Leaping down from the hole was one old woman—a slender witch in a red outfit reminiscent of a nun's habit. Against the pure white backdrop, the contrast was sharp.

Grugell, the Witch of the Midnight Sun. The veteran witch could control snow, a subspecies of the astral power of ice. She was infamous, placing herself on the Imperial soldiers' witch list.

"Persistent, aren't you? Isn't it past your bedtime, Granny?"

"I would love to rest if you'd let me. I'm tired of playing tag." The witch in red raised her hands. "You will give me Miss Sisbell."

"I'm afraid not."

Just as the snow exploded below the witch's feet, Jhin grabbed Sisbell's hand and started to sprint.

"Jhin! The soldiers from earlier are coming again…!" Commander Mismis shouted.

"Don't worry about them, boss. Don't look behind you—*run*!"

Growling behind them were giants made of astral energy. Golems. Jhin had seen ones made from earth before but never ones formed from snow.

"Nene—don't use your gun. You'll be wasting your ammo."

They'd have trouble bringing down the giants. Even if Nene destroyed a part of those things with a pistol or a machine gun, they would regenerate and attack again.

The golems hot on the heels of Unit 907 made the floor quake beneath them.

"Wh-what are we going to do?!" Sisbell asked.

"We can't go to the first floor," Jhin responded. "And we can't outrace them on this floor...which leaves us with the third floor. Go!"

The group scrambled to the staircase. The stairs had been designed for humans, which made them almost inaccessible to the golems.

However...the group of humans were obviously being *led* there.

"...It's like we're being hunted."

The elderly witch slowly walked toward them. They'd thought she was going to let the golems do the chase, but she'd been pursuing them while maintaining her distance. Her feet followed the footprints left by Jhin and the others in the fallen snow. She seemed exactly like a hunter.

"Y'know, Granny, you're getting too old for this kind of thing." As he clambered up the stairs, Jhin breathed out puffs of white in the frozen space. "Who do you think is hunting who? Don't underestimate Imperial soldiers."

3

The Lou Erz mansion. First floor hall.

Sparks crackled. Black smoke, thin as needles, curled toward the ceiling from the right and left walls. All he could see were thick clouds of dust, which caked his lungs. It was the only thing that remained after the walls and ceilings had been destroyed beyond all recognition.

"The Sovereignty is a country that's old—very old."

Like the parting of the sea, a middle-aged man smartly dressed in a white suit emerged from the dust. He had the face of a movie star—on which he wore a mild-mannered, gentlemanly smile—and defined muscles. He was the head of the Hydra, Talisman—a powerful purebred who led one of the three royal houses and was the man behind the coup d'état.

"The queen from the House of Lou is desperate to maintain the stalemate in the war with the Empire. The Zoa are waiting to exact their revenge. The Hydra, you see, are bored with the status quo."

"......"

"What's your view on the matter, Imperial subject?" Talisman asked, his voice soft.

"Wouldn't you like to know?" the Imperial swordsman—Iska—spat in reply. "I don't plan on dragging this conversation out. I'm pretty sure I already told you that."

"Hmm?"

"I already know how you do things. You're just buying time so you can catch Sisbell."

Iska, the former Saint Disciple, had separated from Unit 907 to buy time for Sisbell's escape. He had stayed behind for one reason: the head of the Hydra. Though the man *seemed* mild-mannered at first glance, his genial expression was little more than a mask that he showed the public. In actuality, he was a fiend—and one with extraordinary powers at that.

...One of the Founder Nebulis's descendants—a purebred with the astral power of Waves.

...He's a danger to us all.

Plip. A red droplet landed on Iska's skin.

The wound that he was sure had stopped bleeding earlier had reopened on his forehead. Blood ran along his eyelid from the wound. Before it got into his eyes, Iska used the back of his hand to wipe it away.

CHAPTER 1

"I wonder what you're implying—about me buying time to catch Sisbell."

In that moment...Talisman's figure started to get hazy.

Piles of debris on the floor exploded. As soon as Iska felt something pressing against his skin, he leaped back, exerting all his physical strength.

Fwoom. The air burst. Talisman's fist grazed the tip of Iska's nose before ripping through space. It felt like a train had passed by Iska, whose hair whipped back. His body lifted slightly off the ground.

All that had been caused *just by wind pressure.*

...Does he really only have the astral power of Waves?!

...How much strength does he have concentrated in his fist?!

These waves were surges, which manipulated invisible mechanical energy. This type of astral power itself wasn't too uncommon, but the Imperial forces had determined that it could only shoot shots like invisible bullets.

But Talisman was different. He could accelerate this mechanical energy and power up his bodily constitution.

"Your eyes. They're so observant." Talisman's form disappeared in an instant.

Iska sensed him from above. Before he could come down, the soldier whipped his head up to look at the ceiling.

"Sensed this, too? Is it your hearing? Or touch?"

"Both," Iska answered.

The atmospheric blast created wind. As soon as the breeze caressed Iska's skin, he was in a battle stance before he could even see the man. If he couldn't rely on his eyes, he would figure out his opponent's movements with another sense. That was what his training had been for.

Something detonated.

Talisman had leaped, nearly touching the ceiling, then brought his fist down on the floor of the ancient castle. The result sounded like an aerial bombardment. The stone floor shattered as though gunpowder had exploded.

"Amazing. It's like you have a sonar system from your head to your toes," he commented. Talisman's eyes twinkled with a *smile* while he pursued Iska.

When the swordsman tried to counter, the purebred would come at the Saint Disciple with an attack himself, neutralizing the blow. This was why Iska kept his distance. As soon as Talisman realized that, he paused to brush the dust off his suit.

Spectators would never have realized that as seconds ticked by and they stared each other down, life-and-death maneuvers were playing out below the surface.

"I know I'm repeating myself, but I really don't get it." The middle-aged man fixed the ruffled collar of his suit and shrugged. "Why are Imperial soldiers protecting an important member of Nebulis? Why risk your life to protect her? Just how large is your promised reward?"

"You're the one who attacked first. What's wrong with driving out insurgents?"

"I suppose it's too late to have this discussion, but this is all a misunderstanding." Talisman forced a smile. "This is an estate owned by the Lou. No one would even imagine Imperial soldiers being in a castle owned by our royal family."

"I doubt that. You must've heard about us from Elletear."

"Tsk."

Though it only lasted for a moment, the head of the Hydra narrowed his eyes. Iska stared straight into them. "You've got the wrong idea about us."

CHAPTER 1

There was something Talisman did not know. The youngest princess, Sisbell, had been looking for the traitor in the royal family before this attack had even occurred.

"Elleteaaaaaar!

"I...I don't understand what you're thinking! Are you trying to betray our motherland?!"

The eldest princess, Elletear, had been trying to overthrow the queen. She had already returned to the palace before the Imperial forces started their raid.

...And she went back to the scene to orchestrate it.

...To shepherd the elite troops from the Empire into the royal palace.

This wasn't some short-term scheme. It had been plotted over years—or passed down for generations until it had reached Talisman, and Elletear had given her support to him.

"I'm the one asking the questions. Why did Elletear betray the queen?" Iska continued.

"Hmm?"

"Don't play dumb. I know you're behind all this. You won't be able to get away with it as long as Sisbell is around."

"What do you think of her beauty?"

"...Excuse me?"

Was that supposed to throw him off-balance?

Talisman continued without minding Iska's defensive stance. "If magic existed in this world, it would take the shape of Elletear. A goddess must have doted upon her to make her so beautiful. Her looks are a gift from above."

"......" *What does that have to do with my question?*

Before Iska could ask...

"But the *planet didn't share the same love for her*," declared the head of the Hydra in a cold tone. "It seems you've misunderstood something. She and I do not share the same goal. We want opposite things. We just so happened to have a common means to each of our ends."

"...And that's overthrowing the queen?"

"I think an Imperial subject would agree with me. If the current queen were to disappear, the Sovereignty would be temporarily disarmed. And that might bring the Empire on top in the war."

"Was that how you proposed this to the Empire?"

"I'll leave that to your imagination."

"...I'll answer one question for you." Iska stared at the purebred as if testing the man. He pointed the tip of the black astral sword in his right hand. "This isn't the kind of fight I want to have against the Sovereignty."

"And what makes you feel that way?"

"Nothing will change with the way the Hydra are doing things. It'll just progressively hurt both countries and deepen the divide."

They would strike and counterattack. The strife between the two superpowers would only mount.

...That's not what I want.

...Or how I want things to end.

Iska was a subject of the Empire. He hoped that the end of the war would mean victory for the Empire. But that *didn't* mean he wished for *the downfall of the Sovereignty*. He wanted to end the war by having the Imperial forces capture a member of their royal family, so he could negotiate for peace through the Imperial leaders.

"You're taking things too far. I don't want either the Empire or the Sovereignty to fall."

"Ha-ha. Seems you're a romanticist." The member of the royal family clapped and cackled. "A sweet dream. You're quite the romantic for being such a hell-raiser. Unfortunately, I do believe that all the other Saint Disciples and members of the royal family were waiting for this day to come."

"...What do you mean?"

"It's a pissing match. Haven't we all been wondering who would come out on top for decades?"

The purebred containing potent astral energy—Talisman the Tyrant—opened his arms.

"It's the prided Saint Disciples of the Empire versus the purebreds, descendants of the Founder Nebulis. It's time to determine which will reign supreme. That's what happens tonight."

CHAPTER 2

Night of the Witch Hunt, Part II

1

The Nebulis palace.

A fortress constructed by the Founder Nebulis and other astral mages persecuted in Imperial territory. Comprised of the three spires—the Star, Moon, and Solar—and the Queen's Palace, the castle had four distinct towers known to the Empire. At this moment, an Imperial unit was hatching a plan to invade the Queen's Palace.

"Whoa there! That was close…"

Six inches in front of the Imperial soldiers, the floating glass corridor called the Moon Diadem was caving in, smashing to pieces as they entered the corridor.

"Oof. Construction hazard. If I didn't back away fast enough, I would've been plunging headfirst to the ground. We're practically up as high as a skyscraper here. That was super-scary."

"Gah! …Mei!"

At least one person had been too late. The commanding officer of the unit grasped the edge of the shattering floor and screamed. Any attempts to scramble back up might have made the floor give way further and send the officer hurtling to the ground.

"P-please help me!"

"Now what'll I do with you, Commanderino? Didn't I tell you to get out of the way?" a wild female soldier responded to him with an exasperated smile. The Saint Disciple of the third seat. The Incessant Tempest, Mei.

Though she was small, the arms peeking from her tank top were tough as steel, her long hair in disarray, skin tanned, and glimpses of her long canines peeking from her lips. The gleam in her eyes gave her the look of a large feline predator.

"Sheesh. You sure are helpless."

She grabbed the back of the commanding officer's neck and threw him high into the sky behind her with one hand, tossing the soldier, who was well over two hundred pounds, like he was an empty water bottle.

Thump. He crashed into the corridor.

"Th-thank you ver—"

"You think that saved your life?" a voice called out, ahead of the Imperial troops from the shattering midair corridor. A girl touched down from the glass ceiling into the passageway. "You'll meet your end here, Imperial soldiers. Because I will eliminate you."

A black-haired girl, almost childish. Her dress was sparkly, and her monotone cadence made her seem doll-like.

Kissing Zoa Nebulis IX. That was how she had introduced herself when they first crossed paths. She opened her arms, which was the harbinger of thousands of miniscule needles appearing all over her body.

"I will erase you. Disappear from my presence."

The purple thorns materialized out of thin air, almost looking

CHAPTER 2

like a sea urchin's. They rained down on Mei, humming ominously as they approached her.

"Oh, yikes." Mei leaped, a ferocious smile on her face, and touched the ceiling thirteen feet above her. The floor below was riddled with holes as Kissing's spikes pierced through it.

Had the floor melted away? Or had it simply disappeared?

The Imperial unit held their breath as they watched the terrifying scene.

"Ha-ha. I get it now. So you can erase physical matter."

The only voice that called out was Mei's, incredibly jovial, as she clung onto the chandelier.

"Here I was, thinking you were the space-time interference variety, but it looks like you haven't erased any space. So you interfere with matter with your planetary type of astral power. Isn't that right?"

The needles that had blotted the floor out of existence began to track their prey once again. Mei observed them.

"I've heard witches with second-generation astral power from the planetary core have purple crests. Mind letting me get a look at yours?"

"Alas, I'm a young lady, and I have no intention of exposing any skin."

"Ha. A young lady? That's something coming from you—you almost sound human, when you're a witch with blood on her hands. Is that your way of telling me you wanna *become* human, monster?"

"……"

"I'll rip off that pretty little costume of yours."

Kissing wore a resplendent royal garment, which was exclusively reserved for the descendants of the Founder. It was perfectly tailored to her dainty frame.

"I wanted a purebred sample to play with. I'm gonna tear that cute little dress apart until I get a peek at that astral crest of yours, wherever it is."

"Sounds like a grand time," Kissing replied.

Even as Mei showered the girl with impressive threats, the charming black-haired witch listened, acting like she was comforted by Mei's words.

"Imperial soldiers seem to be just as savage as my uncle On has told me. That works perfectly for me. I won't have to hold back. I can do unspeakable things to you—*disappear, Imperial subject.*"

Her needles combined, forming a whip like a barbed wire. Kissing gripped the lash of thorns and cracked it. As if the whip had a mind of its own, it snaked wildly through the air, coming after the Saint Disciple hanging off the chandelier overhead.

"Silly Imperial subject. I'll have you disappear before you even reach the ground."

Checkmate.

Mei's only option was to kick off the chandelier into the open air, but even if she managed to dodge the crack of the whip, the weapon was made from a cluster of thorns. The whip would trail after her, and the spot where she stood would cease to exist.

"Is that what you think?" Faster than the thorns could prick her, Mei kicked the chandelier as a foothold and launched herself at the witch. "I'll baptize you…in glass."

"Huh?!"

Mei should have had one choice. Observing the entire fight, Kissing and Mei's Imperial soldiers had been convinced of that.

They never would have imagined that this would happen— that she would have *kicked the chandelier*, which weighed several hundred pounds, spraying glass bullets down on Kissing.

The astral power activated its automatic defense. The thorns, which should have been going after Mei, switch direction in an

CHAPTER 2

instant, meeting the shower of glass bullets and erasing every single one of them.

"You used my astral power's defense mechanism *against me*?!"

"What? Oh, you've lived a sheltered life for someone with such strong powers. If you don't know strategy, you're hardly a witch. You sure you're not just a doll?"

The Saint Disciple took her time getting back down to the floor, graceful as a cat. She was nearly silent until she landed, and fragments of glass crunched underfoot.

Mei snapped her fingers. "Or maybe you'll be the one riddled with holes, little miss... Fire."

Gunshots echoed in the corridor. The four Imperial soldiers on standby behind Mei were carrying their automatic TH87 rifles—anti-witch equipment that could shoot six hundred bullets per minute.

Four guns firing forty bullets per second. They could even blast away the anti–astral power riot shields of the astral corps.

"Have you forgotten that I'm a descendant of the Founder?"

All the rounds disappeared into empty air right before they came into contact with Kissing. Hundreds of bullets had been fired at her, which would have pulverized any human, but they vanished like magic.

"...Impossible! But there were so many!"

Ping. The noise signaled they were out of ammo. After using up a magazine, one of the Imperial soldiers froze, fear on his face. Everyone assumed a purebred would be able to defend herself against a spray of bullets, but the Imperial soldier started to panic when he saw it happen in front of him—because Kissing's Thorns had protected her.

Thorns weren't meant to guard anyone against bullets, unlike wind barriers or surges.

To defend herself against forty high-speed bullets per second, she would have needed to snipe every single one. It was like firing hundreds of rounds to shoot down hundreds of enemy bullets. This level of precision wasn't achievable without the most cutting-edge interception systems from the Empire.

"...Are you saying you shot all of them down?!"

"Of course, seeing that I'm of the Zoa."

Purple astral light radiated from Kissing's entire body. Thorns emerged from the light, soaring into the air.

"The Zoa have a method of controlling astral power that Imperial subjects have not encountered from fighting the Lou and the Hydra... Oh, I shouldn't have said that. My uncle On told me not to say a word about that to anyone."

The three bloodlines each had their own field of research. The Zoa were experimenting with berserking and controlling astral power. The Lou and Hydra hadn't been successful in controlling their attacks. While Queen Mirabella and Alice possessed powers that could accidentally be directed toward their allies, Kissing could target only her enemies. She had defended herself from the bullets using that precision control.

"A slip of the tongue. There shouldn't be any issues if I make all who know this secret disappear. In that case..."

Mei got down on one knee to the floor. "Ruined King Hurricane, engage," declared the Saint Disciple of the third seat, the Incessant Tempest. The exposed skin on her shoulder tore open, splattering blood.

Kissing had done nothing. Mei had positioned herself as if she was carrying something, which then made her shoulder ooze with blood like sharp claws had dragged through her skin.

"Uh!" For the first time in her life, the purebred felt something cold tingling through her body. *Something was wrong.*

CHAPTER 2

She could feel with her body that she'd never experienced this kind of threat during her rigorous training arranged by the House of Zoa.

"My thorns, tear that woman apar—"

"It's too late."

That was her death sentence.

The active-camouflage weapon that Mei shouldered returned to its original form and engaged. The once-invisible object transformed into a gigantic battering gun with a dull sheen. An electronic-control-type autocannon, Model 36—the Ruined King Hurricane. The weapon in the shape of a battleship could fire *a thousand bullets per second*, and there was no astral power that could defend against that, be it flames, wind, lightning, ice, water, or earth.

This weapon could annihilate *any* astral mage.

"Did I forget to tell you? My nickname's the Incessant Tempest. I'll teach you why I'm called that." Mei grinned, flashing her sharp canines. Her body seemed to have the charm of a cat and the bloodlust of a lion. "Bye-bye, cute little witch."

Kissing, the Witch of Thorns, heard the roar of the storm as it blew toward her.

Queen's Palace. Midair garden.

The area was blasted by heat waves, carrying the scent of garden flowers, smoke, and cinders, which began to irritate the sinuses of the two people who occupied the space.

"Oops, I almost forgot. Could I ask you one question, lovely Saint Disciple?"

On Zoa Nebulis. Smartly dressed in a black suit, he was one

of the few people allowed to give orders in place of the head of the Zoa, which was one of the three royal bloodlines. Because he hid the old scars on his face under a mask, he had taken on the alias of Lord Mask.

"I neglected to ask something very important. Would you mind telling me how you made your way into the Queen's Palace?"

The door to the Queen's Palace was closed. There were no other Imperial soldiers who had managed to explore beyond its doors. So how had this woman invaded the palace alone?

"Hmm. I would prefer not to reveal my trade secrets." The tall, bespectacled Saint Disciple tilted her head, putting on an act. Then her tone relaxed. "I *don't* dislike your bold questioning of the enemy."

The Saint Disciple of the fifth seat, Risya. Known as the adviser to the Lord Yunmelngen, she had left the Imperial capital of her own volition to fight. That fact alone was enough to show that the Empire meant serious business.

"I'm not asking you to disclose your tricks, but why not give me something to work off of?"

"I'll give you a hint, but that's it. Your front door was closed."

"Okay." Lord Mask On put his hand to his chin as he hummed in a low voice. "In which case, I suppose I'll—"

He winked out of sight. Only his voice was left behind as the masked man slipped into the night like he was melting into darkness.

"Grk."

"—hear the rest from a Saint Disciple's body."

Risya heard him from behind.

He had teleported. The tip of Lord Mask's knife plunged into Risya's back—or it should have.

CHAPTER 2

"What the—?"

"...Whoa. That was close. I thought you might try that."

The tip of the knife cut through air. Lord Mask cried out in surprise as Risya—the Saint Disciple and adviser of the Lord—nimbly circled around him. She seemed to glide backward.

"Oh, I forgot to tell you. I already know about your surprise attacks, unfortunately. Do you remember an Imperial soldier named Mismis by any chance?"

"Mismis?"

"At Mudor Canyon, you kicked a commander into the vortex. Remember? I guess it doesn't matter if you remember." Over her glasses, she stared down her foe. "I was classmates with her, you see, so I've heard plenty about you."

"...Mismis. Oh, now I remember. You mean that petite woman. So that's how you know. That makes sense. Well, my powers don't amount to much, as you might be aware." He tucked his clean knife away into his breast pocket. "Lady Risya, are you telling me that you're the only one who was promoted to Saint Disciple from your cohort of commanders?"

"More or less."

"It seems to me that the pecking order in the Imperial forces is a delicate one. I'm sure someone as talented as you must invite envy from your peers."

"I'm used to it." The Saint Disciple took off her black-rimmed glasses.

Lord Mask wasn't just imagining that her eyes seemed even sharper now that she'd removed her thin frames.

"I mean, this is the *fourth time I've been twenty-two*."

"...Hmm?"

"Oh, but that's a secret between you and me. If anyone were to find out, the Lord would give me an earful." She hooked her finger around a hinge of her glasses, skillfully swinging them around her finger as she grinned.

And it's not like you can use that against me. Her eyes gleamed, provoking him.

"Imperial soldiers apply themselves day in and day out. We must train if we're to face witches and sorcerers."

"This is quite something. I thought you were a young lady, but you're actually an old, seasoned veteran with a long history."

"Oh no, I'm a young lady. *Restarting* life before I reach my thirties is just my way of doing things. I'm a blossoming young lady full of grace." Risya waved her free hand and smiled. "The secret isn't some miracle antiaging drug or plastic surgery. It's much more painful and frightening. If you want to know more, you're welcome to come to the Empire and find out for yourself."

"I'm fine."

"That's a shame. Oh, I know. Based on the task given by the Eight Great Apostles—"

Fwoom. He felt the slightest sense that something was off. Hidden within the evening air that whipped around them, he heard a sound like someone was cutting through space.

"We were told to capture a purebred."

A thread twinkled, thinner than a strand of hair. It had wrapped itself around the masked man's neck. For the first time, the elegant man couldn't hold back the surprise in his voice.

"What?!"

Then he teleported. Risya looked at Lord Mask, who warped just two yards ahead, and the thread of light that had failed to capture its target reeled back into her hands.

"Oh, too bad. I'm impressed you noticed." She moved like a spider after missing her prey by a hair's breadth. The Saint Disciple

CHAPTER 2

smiled bitterly. "Do you know about the carotid sinus reflex? It's the tenderest spot of the human body."

"......"

"Any man, no matter how great, will lose consciousness within five seconds if pressure is applied at the right point on his neck. And since it's painless, it's hard to respond to it before it's too late. If I'd tugged on the thread around your neck just a little quicker, I would have made you drop to the floor. Blame me for being inexperienced."

Lord Mask was silent. The sharpest member of the Zoa realized something about the Saint Disciple's hands. As she continued to spin her glasses, astral light came out of her fingertips.

"Astral powers are so inconvenient. Even the thinnest of threads glow with astral energy, making them easy to detect at night. I wish it was the afternoon."

"......"

"Well, think of this as payback. It's much more civilized compared to how you went around my back—a young lady's back, I might mention—and tried to pierce me with a knife."

Astral energy was an inexplicable force that astral powers discharged. It was not something that humans could produce. Only mages with astral powers were blessed with its use.

So how could a Saint Disciple from the Empire use such a thing?

"Imperial servants really are irredeemable," growled a low voice from behind the mask, stifled, but bone-chilling. "You might condemn us as witches and sorcerers, yet you use astral powers behind our backs. You're the same as us—just in a Saint Disciple's skin..."

"You're directing your anger at the wrong person."

"Hmm?"

"I won't deny that we've been experimenting with how to bond astral powers with humans, but we never could have done it without help from the royal family."

"...So you're saying there are traitors among us." The man in black rapped on the edge of his mask with his fingertip. "The Zoa have already come to that conclusion, but I welcome all information. Why don't you tell me their names while you're at it?"

"Oh, you're so slow." Risya put her glasses back on, looking at the Founder's descendant past her thin lenses. Her mouth curved into a smirk. "Do you really need me to deliver some stodgy line—'I'll tell you if you win against me'—for you to get the hint?"

"Oh, forgive me."

"That's why *you can't escape.*"

Risya In Empire. The Saint Disciple of the fifth seat spread her arms in front of the masked purebred. Star threads appeared from Risya's fists and dispersed into the air, beginning to cover the garden like a spiderweb. This was astral power—fourth-generation Weave. It didn't exist within the Nebulis Sovereignty because this astral power had appeared in a vortex in the Empire's own domain.

"Don't you want to know all my secrets? You don't want to let me out of your sight, right? That's why you could never leave this place."

"That's exactly what I want."

Lord Mask On straightened himself and bowed with perfected grace.

It was like an evening masquerade. In attendance were a gentleman and lady who'd had a chance encounter—their exchange almost like an invitation for a dance.

"A beautiful young lady has called upon me. I wouldn't be a gentleman if I was to decline."

"I won't say I'm not a fan of your theatrics. However..." The adviser of the Lord narrowed her eyes before twisting around in

a fascinating manner and tucking her limbs in close to her body. "I think I might like your unadorned face better. Your true face behind the mask—a hideous, inhuman form. It seems like it would be fitting for a sorcerer."

"Even I don't remember what I look like under it."

"I'll make you show me—even if that means I rip the thing off your face."

Their eyes were like the void as they spoke to each other.

The sorcerer and the Saint Disciple launched off the ground at the same time, as if they were about to dance.

2

Meanwhile…in the Moon Spire, which was connected to the Moon Diadem, the midair corridor leading to the Queen's Palace…

Plink-plink…

Plink… Pebbles hit the floor, special crystals from the ceiling and remains that had made up the walls of the spires until a few seconds ago. These stones were hard enough that mid-grade impacts wouldn't chip their exterior.

And yet, the walls had caved in like a sandcastle, leaving a gaping hole.

That was the work of the electronic-control-type autocannon, Model 36—the Ruined King Hurricane. A single individual-use weapon had dealt this destruction.

"Whew. That packed a punch."

Mei tossed the gigantic autocannon onto the ground. Wielding the weapon on her shoulder had torn through her skin. She was bleeding. The recoil of the gun had forced her feet to dig into the floor.

CHAPTER 2

What was noteworthy wasn't the gun but Mei herself. The soldier had been *carrying the weapon since she had invaded the palace*, invisible because of active camouflage. It was designed to be lighter, but the cannon still weighed a substantial amount. It had originally been made for a warship. Mei had been walking around, jumping, and running, shouldering that weapon the entire time.

Just as the witches and sorcerers had their astral powers, she had been blessed with a gift: peculiar physical makeup.

"Ma'am, um…I believe we were trying to capture the purebred alive…"

"Oh, whoopsie. Got carried away." Mei put on a forced smile.

A mountain of rubble had formed in the corridor, which was clouded with dust. It was difficult to see, even through the scope of a gun.

Anyone hit by a thousand bullets per second wouldn't retain a humanlike form.

"I feel compelled to bully sheltered little girls. I mean, I was born surrounded by gunfire. I survived off muddy water and dug the rot from my festering wounds… The battlefield means life or death. But the purebreds have life different."

By chance, they were born into their powers. That was the only reason they were guaranteed a sheltered life. They could waltz onto the battlefield if they felt like it and beat back Imperial soldiers like they were fleas.

The purebreds looked upon the Imperial soldiers with scorn, as if asking, *Why are you so weak?*

Had the Empire persecuted witches? No.
The witches were the ones looking down on the humans.

* * *

Mei and the soldiers under her command basically lived on the battlefield. They had seen the witches mock the weak humans. Naturally, the Nebulis Sovereignty itself never admitted to this.

Was the Sovereignty after a world that didn't persecute astral mages?

That had to be a lie.

Out of everyone, the Founder's descendants belittled humans the most, even as they extolled such virtues.

"That's what really gets me up in a bunch. Don't you agree, Commanderino?"

"Yes, ma'am. We're only human in this fight."

The Empire had its own idea of justice. The Imperial soldiers—simply human—would dedicate themselves to training before finally being tossed onto the battlefield.

And then…they would be kicked aside by the witches, who had been *born* strong. Rumors of inhuman Imperial weapons might make the rounds, but the soldiers were almost always the ones being hurt by the astral corps.

"Hence why Imperial soldiers use our brains, little miss. That goes for my weapon and our raid. I bet you don't get it, though, seeing as how you've got rose-colored glasses on."

Mei tutted at the pile of rubble. She glanced at her reports, then turned her back to them. She heard the debris clattering before it tumbled away and blasted into the air.

"……"

"Ma'am?"

"Oh, good. We were trying to take one of them alive, after all. I'm glad you're safe."

Mei looked ahead…craning her neck to see the pile of rubble that let out an earsplitting screech as it melted away like ice.

CHAPTER 2

"No!"

"H-how could she be alive after taking those bullets?!"

"Quiet down, Commanderino. Keep back and watch. The astral corps will be gathering any minute because of that gunfire anyway."

Either way, her reports wouldn't be any use to her. If a shot from the Ruined King Hurricane hadn't been enough to stop the purebred in her tracks, any sort of backup fire would hardly serve any purpose.

"Looks like the purebred wasn't unharmed."

"……Uh…ah……" The girl's breath was ragged as she struggled to get out of a hole in the rubble.

Her tailored royal garb had been reduced to tatters. Her white skin, untouched by the sun, had been scraped by debris, leaving it bloody.

Her black hair, like silk, was white with dust.

And most importantly…her cute face was crumpled from fear and pain.

"Ow… Ouch… Is this…my blood…?"

It wasn't that Kissing had never experienced defeat. Against the Imperial swordsman Iska, she'd sustained an unexpected loss. This Saint Disciple Mei, however, had something that he had not.

Anger. The wrath of thousands—tens of thousands of Imperial soldiers—toward the witches.

They didn't want peace. Kissing hadn't felt such animosity in her battle with Iska. She hadn't sensed that he wanted all witches to be wiped out.

At this moment, she'd learned something new, *the nature of war*.

"…Uncle On, I think I understand now." Her eyes glittered but not from a change in character.

CHAPTER 2

Kissing's eyes were literally glittering in front of the soldiers.

"Whoa. I see. I was wondering why I wasn't seeing your astral crest even after your clothes were ruined. So your astral crest is in *your eyes*."

Her astral crest glittered behind her eyes. When Kissing had made her entrance, she had covered them with a blindfold. Even the Empire had no information that astral crests could be in such a place. She had to be a rarity even among purebreds.

"Now that's piqued my interest. I'd like you as a sample all the more."

"......" Kissing suddenly stood up and touched the cut on her cheek. She looked down at the red droplets on her fingertips. "I've realized something. War isn't a good thing, not in the slightest. Continuing this would be a waste of time. Particularly seeing as how it's so painful."

"Oh? Had a change of heart?" Mei quipped back.

"Yes. Let's end this war." The girl in her shredded dress spread her arms toward the sky that stretched behind her. Her eyes radiated murder. "By eliminating all the Imperial forces!"

The air whined.

In a few seconds, thorns materialized in the sky, blotting out the light. It was a march of thorns—the Whole of Destruction.

There were hundreds of thousands of them, enough to wipe out an airship and maybe even the Moon Spire. They circled overhead, instantly spreading over Mei and the soldiers.

"What?!"

"...Huh. Now that's quite a look on your face."

The girl was *seething*.

She had lost control. Nothing was keeping her from destroying the Moon Spire, nor did she fear death.

Kissing was a purebred. She'd taken on the form of one of the

47

monsters that the Empire had never once been able to capture in history.

"Ma'am! We're surrounded by her astral attack!"

"I have eyes. Get your butt into gear, Commanderino. You've gotta kill or be killed."

"Do you think you can kill me? I won't show you a shred of mercy," warned Kissing.

All the thorns had spread out to create a barrier. Because of their number, Mei couldn't wipe them out with a barrage from the Ruined King Hurricane.

The Saint Disciple, however, smiled ferociously.

"'Mercy,' you say? Still haven't learned your lesson?"

"...?"

"Don't get excited just 'cause you survived one hit."

The Ruined King Hurricane was still on the ground as the Saint Disciple traced the surface of it with her fingertips.

"You want to hear me predict the future? The next time you hear gunfire will be the last."

"Yes, the last for you, Imperial soldiers." Kissing sounded confident as she made her thorns soar into the air.

Mei let another feral grin slip onto her face, certain of victory.

Who was bluffing? Neither of them. The Saint Disciple and the purebred were convinced of their win.

They both moved at the same time…Kissing producing all thorns possible to send Mei's way, Mei aiming the Ruined King Hurricane with its bullets.

Neither had a chance to fire.

Dark-purple creatures that the Imperial soldiers had never seen before tore into the floor, taking the impact of Kissing's thorns.

CHAPTER 2

"...Huh?!"
"What?!"

The six-legged beasts didn't dissolve into nothing even as they were engulfed in Kissing's thorns. They didn't belong to the Empire. The creatures bared their teeth at both Mei and Kissing before pouncing, mouths split open to their jaws and saliva glowing like astral power dribbled from them. Upon falling to the floor, the drool sizzled, corroding the ground.

Shiver. Mei's sixth sense—saving her from the brink of death—picked up a threat she could not describe.

Was it a grudge? It reminded her of the very rare astral power of Curses, but she couldn't tell if it was. The fact that the things could take Kissing's thorns and remain unscathed was the strangest development of all.

"Kind of seems dangerous. Guess we all have to make a break for it!"

Mei leaped back. The four soldiers didn't try to argue with her.

"Hey, little miss, this thing, it's—"

"Don't tell me it's...Grandfather Growley's astral power!" Kissing turned around, blood draining from her face.

The purebred deploying astral power out of anger faced the beasts.

"Wait, Grandfather, these Imperial soldiers are my—"

From out of nowhere came the ominous howl of the beasts.

3

The heads of the three royal families were the most dependable figures, as they served as figurehead of their bloodlines.

So what made them so reliable?

"To be the strongest astral mage. To be ingenious. To have walked many lives. The requirements are terribly clear."

"And what does it mean to be a queen?"

"It's not so different from the head of household. If you must press me to say something about her, I suppose favorability in the polls is another factor." The elderly man in the wheelchair chuckled hoarsely.

The head of the Zoa, Growley. His face was afflicted by wrinkles and old age. Though he was a man over seventy, his voice was surprisingly full and his eyes gleamed fiercely.

"If a beautiful young girl with strong astral powers becomes queen, that's enough to give the citizens hope."

"Sounds like you're dissatisfied. Are you mad that you're a man who can never be queen?"

"Nonsense. We don't have qualms with the abilities of our current queen. I'm impressed with how the war automatons—hopeless things thirty years ago—have turned *so human*."

The Moon Spire in the Nebulis Sovereignty—a gigantic three-story space illuminated by a light fixture modeled after the full moon and with a multipurpose hall used for events.

On this evening, it had been visited by one of the Empire's prided assassins.

"That's right. She was similar to you: like the cold edge of a bloodthirsty sword and a barrier that prevented anyone from coming near her. A marionette for war."

"Your queen? Similar to me? Ha! I'd rather you not lump me in with a witch. Even I pride myself as a human. We're different from you." The Imperial subject snorted. He was the Saint Disciple of the eighth seat, the Invisible Hand of God, Nameless.

His form seemed to wink in and out of sight, seeing that he was clothed from head to toe in a dark-gray coat. He could make

CHAPTER 2

himself disappear with active camouflage, a master at silent killing without guns.

"In the old days, I mean. A time when you were a newborn or not of this world."

Creak, the old man turned his wheelchair slightly.

"Back when she was fourteen or fifteen. That had been her prime—when she was a silent, bloodthirsty killer. During those two years, she was the most powerful queen candidate in all history... Now, her fangs have dulled. Maybe as a consequence from departing the battlefield since becoming the queen or a mother."

"What are you trying to say?"

"It's time to *change dynasties.*" There was power in Growley's words. "I'm grateful to the Imperial forces. The blame will lie on the queen who has invited chaos. In the coming conclave, the House of Lou will fall—leaving only the Sun and Moon."

He pointed at the Saint Disciple bathed in light.

"So the Imperial forces have served their purpose. Perish."

Shadows burst from the old man's feet. Sprays of purple light flooded the hall before condensing and turning into baying six-legged hounds.

"Did you materialize astral energy?"

"These are avatars. You're already guilty of a crime. That crime has become your punishment."

The old man pulled out an iron rod that was embedded in his shoulder, an assassination weapon that resembled the tip of an ice pick. When they had encountered each other minutes ago, the old man had *purposefully* let Nameless throw the weapon and hit him.

"You became my enemy as soon as you attacked me. Can you escape from your own Vice?"

"Vice? I'm not planning to atone for anything." Nameless swung one of his hands up. With an underthrow, he flung another iron

rod. As soon as it touched the ceiling, sparks scattered above Growley's head.

A small bomb buried in the rod had denotated. A panel in the ceiling came crashing down and crushed the avatars directly below.

"That does nothing."

The creatures that had been pinned under the panel crawled out.

"Nothing physical will affect these avatars. Even Imperial missiles wouldn't be able to defeat them. Isn't your left arm proof of that?"

"Are they counteroffensive astral powers?" Nameless shielded his immobile left arm and leaped back.

That had come out of the conflict from two minutes before.

He'd attempted to punch an avatar with his left fist as it tried to attack him, but the thing had passed right through him and possessed his arm. It had turned into a curse—corroding away at his arm.

What was Vice?

Just what kind of astral power did this sorcerer have?

"The astral energy reacts to its enemies and evolves. Once it's grown past a certain point, it takes on the form of a beast to attack. To evolve, it needs the enemy to hurt it... No, that can't be the only condition. There are multiple things that can trigger its growth. So that's what this Vice is?"

"I don't intend to reveal my tricks. I will commend you for being on the right track, however." Growley smiled like he was snarling. "How about I share one secret with you? These creatures grow indefinitely."

"An objectionable astral power. Don't you think it's counterproductive that it can phase through matter?"

The silent killer kicked off the ground, touching the barrier

CHAPTER 2

at the very back of the hallway and ricocheting up, leaping wall to wall. Over the heads of the avatars chasing after him, Nameless raised his right hand.

He held a ceramic knife.

At full speed, Nameless could throw as fast as a gun. The first time, he had aimed for the old man's shoulder to see what would happen. This time, he aimed for the man's chest.

The avatars wouldn't be affected by anything physical. In other words, the knife would pass right through them, doing nothing to stop their advance.

"Disappear, sorcerer, right along with your astral power."

"With the blooming of flowers comes the wind and rain... Before things can go your way, something will *get* in your way, youngster."

The knife stopped.

An arm from another avatar shot out from under the wheelchair, catching the blade that Nameless had thrown. It looked like a human hand.

"...*What?!*"

"You can't affect them through physical interference. But they *can* interact with matter. Do you understand what that means, youngster?"

The Imperial Saint Disciple landed on his feet. *"It's as if you're claiming you're invincible."*

"That's *precisely* what I am saying."

The avatars couldn't be beat. On top of them coming to attack in packs, they turned into an ultimate shield, protecting the old man from any type of physical assault. This was the astral power of Vice.

This counteroffensive power that Growley maintained could turn into something ridiculous once its conditions were met.

"So basically, you and your creatures can't ever be hurt by your enemy's attacks. Only you can attack your opponents."

"Indeed."

"Now that's pretty absurd. Seems to me like there'd be some loophole."

"There is none. Because of that, I'm invincible. Imperial bombs, poison gas, missiles—none of them can defeat me. The proof of that is these seventy years."

"............"

"To be crowned head of household isn't just titular, you know."

Growley controlled the Zoa.

None of the bombings of the past had come close to defeating this old man. That was the reason Lord Mask and Kissing idolized him.

"If only my legs could move. I would have turned the Imperial capital to ash fifty years ago."

"*We should be in awe of the younger generation. How can we know what they are planning to do?*" recited the Imperial subject.

"...What?" The old man was surprised. He narrowed his eyes dubiously. It was an old idiom. Why would the youth of today know the words of a great man of the past?

Any form of past glory would be overwritten in the future. The maxim mocked the old man who boasted seventy years of battle experience. It was the opposite of Growley's previous quote: "With the blooming of flowers comes wind and rain."

"*You say that would have happened if only your legs were mobile? You exaggerate your former glory. You've become old, sorcerer.*"

Nameless's left arm, cursed by the avatar, was still slack and unable to so much as twitch. The Saint Disciple of the eighth seat leaped off the ground once again, fast enough to leave an afterimage as he jumped to the side. By a paper-thin margin, he dodged the silent avatar pursuing him from behind.

CHAPTER 2

"I admit your astral power is extraordinary. However..."

The sorcerer might have purported that the queen's fangs had dulled, but he, too, was held captive by his old age.

"Your astral power might have remained the same. But hasn't its wielder gotten old?"

"Ha!" Growley laughed. Marked with age spots, his face contorted, and his lips formed a bemused sneer. "I thought you were just an assassin, but it seems you're more than that. I haven't seen one like you in a while. *Someone who can hold a decent conversation?* Tell me your name."

"I have no name to offer a monster. Haven't I already told you that?"

"I'm asking you for your name again. That doesn't happen often."

"Has your hearing been affected?"

"How rude." The elderly man did not hide his joyful tone. "But you cannot prevail over death simply through spirit."

Behind Nameless, the avatars began to inflate. Vice would grow infinitely. The beasts—once hip level, the size of dogs—spouted three heads and grew tall enough that even the Saint Disciple had to crane his neck to look at them.

"Looks exactly like Cerberus. How big do these things get?"

"Until you exhaust your strength. The greatest record was… about as big as this Moon Spire, I suppose."

The Cerberus had grown large enough to crush Nameless and seemed dreadfully agile. Congealed astral energy, it remained silent. However…

"Hmm…" Growley doubted his own eyes. They couldn't catch him. The avatars that had continued to pursue Nameless couldn't even catch up to a Saint Disciple—a single human.

Just in the same way that Growley was a threat to the Imperial forces, this man was unmistakably a danger to astral mages everywhere.

"If I crush you, then all my vices or whatever will disappear, right?"

Nameless had been approaching the old man with a readied fist. Under his feet, the floor bounced like a rubber ball.

"So they propagate?"

"They don't just grow. Your vices will continue to breed."

From under Growley's wheelchair, new avatars crawled out in the shape of lions. They were even larger than the Cerberus. Nameless had lions to his front and the Cerberus to his back.

He *couldn't* manage to escape.

If any part of his enemy touched Nameless, he would corrode from the curse. If it touched his head, that would spell instant defeat. As soon as he realized that, he acted quickly, spinning himself like a top. The acceleration raised his immobilized left arm—into the mouth of the lion that bared its teeth at him.

"You can have it." He let them chew on his left arm.

Making the lion close its mouth, Nameless let his left arm tear off from the shoulder without a sound before the curse could spread across his body.

"...So you abandoned it!"

"It's an artificial arm."

He'd lost it in a battle to the death with a certain mage.

All Imperial soldiers risked their lives. Every Saint Disciple had wandered the boundary of life and death at least once. That was what it took to challenge a purebred.

And now...in exchange for losing his left artificial arm, Nameless stepped toward Growley's throat.

"—Gh!"

The Saint Disciple's fist tried to ram into Growley.

An avatar caught that punch. A giant in humanoid form crawled out from under the wheelchair like the walking dead.

"...*What?*"

CHAPTER 2

"A second crime. You've become a second-time offender by trying to attack me. A repeat offense is more sinful, you know."

The seven vices: surprise attacks, repeat offenses, use of weapons, outnumbering the opponent, destruction, deception, and betrayal.

Nameless had committed the first two. The "surprise attack" of the iron rod in Growley's shoulder and the "repeat offense."

Because of that, Vice multiplied in that moment.

"Be engulfed by your sins."

Five giants reached toward Nameless. The Cerberus and lion dove toward him. The Saint Disciple confronting them had lost his left arm. His right fist had been desecrated by the curse, left immobilized.

"*Tsk.*"

The ballooning avatars were about to crush him, but right before they could…the highest-ranked combatant from the Empire tsked in irritation and swung his right leg up. He brought it down on the floor.

"You fool. Do you believe the avatars will falter—?"

"*They will.*"

Nameless's heel aimed for the object lying on the ground—his own left arm. He stamped on the mechanism that made up his artificial arm and broke it to pieces himself.

A flash of light.

The last trick embedded in his artificial arm had denotated and flooded the hall in light.

"…Is this an anti–astral power grenade?"

"*So physical interference doesn't work on them. But something that obstructs astral power could.*"

The avatars around Nameless stopped moving.

The grenade could disturb the wavelengths of astral power

over a thirty-yard radius. The only catch was that it was active for exactly two seconds.

The Saint Disciple passed by the avatars surrounding him in a split second and sprinted to the back of the large hall.

"I've seen your astral power. I'll stop it when I see you next."

"You think I'll let you escape?"

The Cerberus pounced, chasing Nameless. The giants were hounding after him, ripping apart the walls and ceiling of the spire. They sprang toward the fleeing man.

The only one left behind in the space was the head of house Growley.

"……"

He checked to make sure the Saint Disciple had left the great hall.

"…I didn't intend to fumble this. That was disrespectful, Imperial soldier."

The old man spat blood as he tumbled from his wheelchair.

The fist that had struck his chest had smashed his rib cage. He wheezed, using every ounce of strength in him to get back onto his seat.

"You can't escape. Vice will continue to pursue you to the ends of the Sovereignty."

Even the head of the Zoa, Growley, had no way of knowing, however…that the Sovereignty had already begun to collapse, with the palace at its core.

4

The Queen's Palace.

One central tower loomed over the palace made of the Star, Moon, and Solar Spires. A fortress for the queen.

CHAPTER 2

The place was a living labyrinth constructed by astral power. Corridor exits shifted based on the month and day. Every floor had an elevator only operable via astral energy. Even if the Imperial army invaded, they wouldn't be able to make a single elevator move.

Raiding it should have been impossible.

All in the Sovereignty had trusted the Queen's Palace for a hundred years.

It was time to destroy their century-long beliefs.

The Queen's Space.

A quiet place decorated with wine-colored carpets, currently buffeted by intense blasts from outside the windows. It was a shadow of its former glory. The near-freezing evening winds and embers burned the skin.

Amid the chaos…

"Oh, Nebulis Queen," called out an Imperial assassin, voice echoing through the Queen's Space.

Technically, it would be imprecise to label one of the Lord's guardsmen an assassin.

"I don't intend to draw this out. Besides, the Astrals will be here in minutes. All the more reason to hurry."

The Saint Disciple of the first seat. The "Flash" Knight, Joheim. Red haired and burly, he wore a personalized battle coat integrated with armor. He took a step forward.

A single step.

As soon as Queen Nebulis IIX recognized that, her bangs blew into disarray.

A change in wind pressure? From that single step?

"Go into eternal rest, right here, right now."

He brought down his narrow blade.

He had teleported—or so it had seemed as the swordsman pursued her. It almost looked like an illusion.

The queen opened her eyes wide, crying out, "Fire!"

It was an air shot.

A mass of air had been gathering at the ceiling. As if activated by a witch's incantation, it turned into a bullet that came crashing down, gouging a hole in the floor.

The air current turned into an invisible wall that shielded the queen. She hurried to the second-floor landing. The Saint Disciple was pushed back to the doors of the Queen's Space, wind sweeping across the room.

"*Mira, the Silent Wind.* Your powers are violent for such a nickname."

"You're stuck decades in the past." She looked down upon the Imperial swordsman from the landing.

Queen Mirabella Lou Nebulis IIX fixed her disheveled bangs with her hand. She kept herself from putting a hand to her chest. Her heart beat wildly, warning her. It didn't need to be put into words: She was agitated from the Saint Disciple managing to get close to her with a single step.

"Mirabella Lou Nebulis IIX—you can manipulate the atmosphere, a wind type of astral mage. You don't control the wind. You control the air," said the Imperial swordsman emotionlessly as if reading from a report. "You headed to the battlefield at the age of eleven. In the ten subsequent years, you gained 3 percent of the Imperial territory. Your appearance on the battlefield was frequent, even for a purebred. You have exemplary physical skills and assassination capabilities for a witch. Eyes were on you as the greatest queen candidate in history and prodigy in the Sovereignty."

"……"

"But you're in *decline*."

He wasn't provoking her. He was just making his observations as the Saint Disciple of the first seat.

"Your strength came from your time on the battlefield as an emotionless war automaton. Now you manufacture smiles as the queen in front of the people. Even steel will rust when all it does is sit in yawn-inducing meetings."

"You speak as if these imagined situations have been witnessed, Imperial subject."

"I have." His long thin sword swished. "Through those living in the castle."

"Oh, really?" Queen Mirabella couldn't care less.

There was a traitor in their midst. She already knew it was someone close to her. In her heart, she could even guess *which daughter* it was.

"It's all a process of elimination."

In a hall occupied by only the two of them, Queen Mirabella's voice called out to him.

"I do not care whether my own abilities are in decline. If I can protect the Sovereignty as its queen, that's the correct choice."

Behind the Imperial swordsman were the ruins of the door that had been sliced into dice-shaped pieces.

...*Why haven't my guards come?*

...*Those nearby should have come running straight here when they heard the roar.*

Generally speaking, there were two defense systems in the Queen's Palace.

The Astrals were the protectors of important figureheads, which included the queen. The other was the commando unit, the Rulers, which hunted invaders. They were true masters at their occupations.

CHAPTER 2

That not a single one of them had appeared showed beyond a doubt that something was clearly wrong here.

...*Did this swordsman beat the guards in front of my door?*

...*Or have other Saint Disciples entered the Queen's Palace and are currently engaging them?*

As she focused on every little movement made by her opponent, she thought of one person. Not any of her guards but her middle daughter Aliceliese. Only seventeen, she was unmistakably the trump card of the Lou when it came to battle. She should have arrived at the palace by now.

"Are you intending to wait for the arrival of the Ice Calamity Witch?"

"What?!"

He'd figured out her hand. Mind blank from shock, the queen stopped thinking for a moment.

Joheim's form flickered. Launching himself from the ground with a kick powerful enough to rock the room, the swordsman moved to the space in front of her eyes, like he was floating.

"Did you use my own trick on me?!"

Bomb Cyclone.

A meteorological term that indicated a rapid change in low barometric pressure. Queen Mirabella's technique created an invisible mine that dragged its prey into a typhoon-level vortex. At full capacity, it could even disarm an Imperial tank. Had he predicted the wind forming from it and cut through the air with his sword?

Impossible.

Master swordsman or not, he wouldn't be able to respond to the queen's attack without knowing her strategy.

"So there *was* a conspirator...!"

"It's information warfare. I wasn't planning on directly attacking you."

"It was *Elletear*, wasn't it?"

The swordsman was silent.

He simply swung his blade down straight at her. As the winds that made up the barrier around Queen Mirabella picked up speed, the Saint Disciple's sword continued forward, tearing through the air.

She felt a cold shiver run through her.

At that moment, something hard passed by her face. Blood sprayed from her cheek.

"Ow!"

How deep had he cut her?

Was it a graze? Or had he cut deeper into her flesh? She wasn't even given time to figure out the extent of her wound. She used all her strength to leap away.

He was quick. That wasn't an accurate way of describing the swordsman.

He was outrageously fast.

If he were simply quick, he wouldn't have been able to overcome her wind barrier. His agility and strength were perfectly balanced, affording him a shocking level of mobility.

"Prepare yourself."

"—Are you sure you're not severely misjudging what I can do?"

They stopped.

Queen Nebulis IIX hadn't used her astral power, and yet Joheim abruptly halted as he stepped onto the landing.

Her eyes twinkled. Had her daughters Alice or Sisbell been there, they would have doubted their eyes. There was the inhuman gleam in the gaze of Mirabella Lou Nebulis IIX—purebred and machine. It was a look she'd never shown her daughters.

CHAPTER 2

"...How unfortunate. It seems the guards and Alice are still not here."

Her clothes rustled as they snaked down her body. She had shed the outer coat that had covered the shoulders of her royal dress. She stripped down to the lightweight bulletproof and blade-proof armor below.

"I don't want to be responsible for destroying the Queen's Space."

Creak. The ominous sound that echoed around Mirabella Lou Nebulis IIX was from the air created by the atmosphere stirring from her astral power. It was the release of her powers that she'd been holding back.

"And here is how it ends."

"......"

The Saint Disciple took the queen's declaration silently.

A murmur escaped from the man. "It seems you don't understand...who I am."

Nothing could have held greater pity and contempt than his sigh.

CHAPTER 3

Night of the Witch Hunt, Part III

1

The Lou Erz mansion.

Gunfire rang out. Sparks flashed from the broken window.

Sounds of combat reached outside the grounds. It was enough to garner the attention of the citizens who shuddered at the Imperial force's advance.

They were stirring.

Outside the grounds of the Lou Erz mansion, the military police came running.

"An Imperial raid?! All the way out here?!"

"We heard gunfire... Don't tell me they're attacking the queen's villa!"

Witness reports came flooding in. People who looked like Imperial forces had traveled by road to attack the mansion.

"—Things have mostly settled outside of this castle."

* * *

Lou Erz mansion. First-floor hall.

The head of the Hydra, Talisman, walked along the dusty floor.

"Since this property belongs to the Lou, the surrounding residences are occupied by citizens who adore the Lou family. I imagine they witnessed armed Imperial soldiers storming this castle."

"I assume they didn't just happen on the scene. You led them there."

Iska glared into Talisman's gentle eyes. He was a demon in the skin of a gentleman. The man leading the coup d'état specialized in throwing his enemies off by speaking to them like this. Even now...

"The details don't matter. What's important is the witnesses will believe that the queen's villa was attacked by Imperial forces. Because that's the reality."

He reached his hand into his breast pocket. The head of the Hydra produced a small communications device. Iska recognized it. It was made in the Empire.

"Come dawn, the Sovereign people will be furious. At the Imperial army—and the current queen's administration who allowed them to invade."

"......"

"Oh, are you interested in this communications device? It's an imitation created to look like it was made in the Empire. I was speaking to my personnel before I came to this abode, you see. I have no use for this anymore."

He threw it down on the ground. Even this seemingly meaningless action was calculated. If an Imperial communications device was left in the villa, it would serve as yet another piece of evidence that the Empire had invaded.

CHAPTER 3

"Well, then. If you'll excuse me, I'll be heading out," Talisman said.

"...What did you say?" Iska knit his eyebrows together. "What do you mean? Sisbell is still—"

"Wouldn't it be odd for a member of the royal family to be absent when the palace is attacked by the Imperial army?" He righted his suit lapel. "You were cornered *from the start*," declared the demon playing the part of a gentleman. "How many years do you think we spent laying this plan out? There was a chance that things wouldn't work out, even if I came to this abode. Well, it's best to be cautious. Depending on the circumstances, Alice might have been here instead of you."

"......"

"Saint Disciple Iska, you did well, just the four of you. I bow my head to you for your gallant effort to protect Sisbell. But we've accomplished our goal."

Iska was silent.

...What does that mean?

...Have they already kidnapped Sisbell? Or is this another one of his strategies?

He had no way of figuring it out now. Because of that...

"You think I'd let you escape?" Iska pointed at Talisman's neck with the tip of his black astral sword. "After all this gunfire and detonations, it wouldn't be odd for the military police to come bursting in here. What do you think they would think if they saw you?"

"They'd realize I'm the mastermind behind everything here."

"So that's the real reason you're trying to get out of here. You intend to escape before the citizens around the castle see you."

That was why Iska wouldn't let him run off. The head of the Hydra was here. If that came out into the open, it would be an easy way to bring down their plan.

"I wonder if that's true?"

Clatter-clatter. Tap... Under Talisman's feet, the rubble on the floor started to move.

Over two hundred pounds of debris scattered along the wall and chandelier fragments snaked along the floor.

"What's this?!"

"You have good instincts. You've realized this isn't my doing and have your guard up. You're right. This isn't my astral power."

The astral power of Waves specialized in brute force, destroying things by crushing and blowing them away. It wasn't something that could draw so much rubble toward him. The fragmented mass crawled along the ground, heading to the broken door behind Talisman and outside to the garden.

...What's going on?

...This isn't the first time I've seen this. I feel as if I've seen something like this before.

Iska couldn't redirect any amount of his focus to think about it. If he was distracted, he wouldn't be careful enough around Talisman himself.

"I said I was communicating with my personnel, but I suppose I should make an addition." The head of the Hydra stomped on the communications device on the ground. His voice was jubilant. "Just earlier, a witch who had been imprisoned for high treason escaped the palace jail. I was speaking with her."

"A witch?"

There were two meanings to that word. In the Empire, it was a derogatory term for astral mages. When an astral mage called someone a "witch" or "sorcerer," they meant a "felon."

"You know this young lady yourself. Haven't you realized it with your instincts, too?"

CHAPTER 3

"...What did you say?"

"You did defeat her once. Unfortunately, if the inquisition thought they could restrain her in an isolated room, they were terribly mistaken. Especially in the state of chaos that the palace is in. After all, she's no longer human. She's a *witch* in the truest sense."

Clatter...clatter-clatter.

Even as Talisman pieced together his words, bulky pieces of debris were being drawn out of the castle.

Was it some form of magnetism? It was like an immense *gravitational force* was pulling things toward it.

A witch. Gravity. Who was associated with such terms...?

"No!"

"Farewell, romanticist." The head of the house Hydra, Talisman, flipped his suit open as he quickly turned around and leaped through the door.

This was bad.

The worst-case scenario worked its way out from Iska's mind—but it wasn't of the mastermind escaping. It was about the rubble that was being dragged away. He had seen that astral power invoked before.

"Uh, wai—"

"Finish it, Vichyssoise."

The ultimate cannon. Magic Shot of Corpses.

All the wreckage from the great hall of the ancient castle combined and compressed to create a bullet that blew away the first floor of the Lou Erz mansion, Iska and all.

The Lou Erz mansion. Third floor.

Chased by snow golems up the stairs, Jhin and the rest of Unit 907 found a pure-white scene of snow before them.

This was the doing of Grugell, the Witch of the Midnight Sun.

The inside of the old castle was piled high with snow like a mirage, but looks were deceptive. There was no way it would be just any old snow.

"...The assassins aren't here. Did they withdraw?"

"Jhin, behind you! Watch out for the golem!" Nene yelled from the rear.

The golem on the staircase made the place shake as it thundered up the steps to the third floor.

"Run to the back."

"I—I know! I know, so please don't let go of my hand!" Sisbell gripped his hand like her life depended on it.

As soon as Jhin and Sisbell, the first two in line, stepped into the snow, the sniper felt an intense pain shoot through his ankle.

"Ouch! Stop! Nene! Boss! You can't step into this snow!"

"Wh-why not?!"

"You don't feel anything?"

"No, so what's—? Eek!" Sisbell's voice cracked when she looked at Jhin's buried leg. The fluffy surface was slowly being stained red.

"*The snow bit me.* If I hadn't been wearing shoes made in the Empire with metal plates in them, it would've torn my foot off, shoe and all."

He endured the pain as he pulled out his foot. The bloodied snow clinging to his shoe had turned into solid, glass-like crystal fragments.

"I-it's like walking through a mountain of needles!" Sisbell cried.

CHAPTER 3

"I know that. It's time for some sleuthing. Why was I the only one who got hurt by the snow? Why're you unharmed?"

"Huh?! Umm..." Sisbell stared at the wintry scene ahead of her and knit her brows. "Creations of astral power will sometimes react based on the absence of said energy. The elevators and doors at the palace— Oh, I—I shouldn't have said that. Pretend you didn't hear me."

"Just keep going."

"S-so this snow only attacks those without astral powers!"

"Then we haven't got a problem. Hey, boss, you're up."

"...I knew you'd make me do this! C'mon! You can't treat your commander like that!"

Mismis rushed out ahead of them and kicked up the fallen snow as hard as she could. Mismis could do it. She pushed away the snow that Jhin and Nene couldn't even touch.

"Keep it up, boss. Just kick the snow that's in the way... I guess I should focus on this first."

Something roared in the passageway. Jhin turned around to face the golem that was crawling up the stairs.

"It's a real shame—I wanted to save this for later."

"You can't, Jhin. Bullets won't work on a golem made from astral pow—"

"Then I guess I'll burn the thing."

"Huh?"

Jhin threw something. As soon as the golem hit and shattered the thing that soared toward it, the smell of alcohol filled their nostrils. Sisbell smelled it sharply in her nose.

"Is that liquor?!"

"A rectified spirit from the banquet table. I borrowed a bottle."

It was 93 percent distilled alcohol and only a beverage in name.

Even the slightest flame would have set it ablaze, making it as flammable as gasoline.

"Too bad you were born a doll made from snow."

Jhin chucked a lighter at the golem. It ignited the alcohol. The giant was engulfed in blistering red flames. The fire even melted the snow around it.

On the other hand…

"…You've gotta be kidding."

Jhin didn't even have time to celebrate. From within the quivering flames, the pile of snow condensed, from which new snow soldiers were born. It wasn't a golem. They were dolls, each about as big as Nene. Now smaller in size, they made up for this difference with their quickness as they started to run toward the flames.

"…So they're planning on forcing their way through the blaze to attack us."

"Jhin, over here! No one's in this room in the very back!" At the end of the hallway, Mismis opened the door to a room and beckoned them in.

The traces of her footprints were left in the snow—the only spots they could cross in this passageway.

"Nene, trace her footsteps and make sure you don't touch the snow."

"I already know that, Jhin." Nene raced through the hall, only stepping in Mismis's tracks. Once she got to the room, she signaled to everyone with her eyes. "Get in, guys! We're closing the door!"

As soon as Jhin leaped into the room, he locked the door from the inside. He leaned against the wall and held his breath.

"D-do you think we can hide in here…?!" Sisbell asked, shoulders heaving.

"Who knows? We haven't got a guaranteed way of escape no matter what we do," he answered gravely. They were cornered.

CHAPTER 3

They might have managed a landing from the second-floor window, but an amateur would have trouble leaping from the third floor. "We've got only one option to escape—*if* we do something about that old lady and get back to the second floor. And *if* we can manage to evade the other soldiers, we might be able to jump into the garden from an open window."

"That seems like quite a few *ifs*!" Sisbell cried.

"Shhh." Nene grabbed her shoulders from behind, making her body shudder.

Crunch. Footsteps were crossing the snow.

It was the snow dolls that had survived the flames—but the issue was their number. It sounded like an entire army was marching toward them.

"...I have to hand it to her. The old lady is persistent. Looks like she's trying to grow her numbers as large as she can."

Bullets wouldn't work against the snow dolls. Mobilized by astral power, their physical strength far outpaced the humans'. If one of them pinned Jhin, he wouldn't be able to shake it off.

"Oh? Are you hiding in a room?"

They could hear the sneer of the old woman from beyond the door that stood between them. She sounded like a witch from a fairy tale. Her hoarse voice was spine-chilling.

"Snow isn't the same as the earth. You might think you can melt a snow golem. Don't you know that astral powers of earth can only be activated where there's dirt? That's the difference with my powers. I can make it snow anywhere."

Crunch, crunch... Dolls in tow, the old woman slowly progressed forward along the snowy floor.

"This is a world of snow. Take a look. I commend you for getting through this scene, but I can see *exactly* where you headed from your footprints."

"—!"

"—Zip it." Jhin clamped down on Sisbell's mouth as she almost started to make a sound.

The footprints continued all the way down the corridor. They could imagine it in the backs of their minds—Grugell the witch pointing at the prints that stopped at the door as she grinned, eyes squinting.

"You locked yourselves away in that room, trying to figure out a way to jump from the third floor outside into the garden before your pursuer gets to you? Well, I suppose that's all you *can* do, but I won't let you have the time to do it. That's what these dolls are for."

Her presence felt almost volatile.

"Do it. Break that door open!"

The snow troops rammed themselves into the door. After dozens of them charged at it, sections of the door exploded. The dolls squeezed themselves through the hole into the room, tumbling in like an avalanche.

"Crush those Imperial soldiers. Leave only Miss Sisbell— Miss...... Huh...?"

They weren't there. Not a single person was in the lounge area of the bedroom. Even the bath and restroom were empty.

"They couldn't have! They couldn't have leaped outside right at that moment..."

"We're *behind you*, Granny."

"...No!" The old woman's entire body shivered when she heard the footsteps of the Imperial soldiers behind her.

Why? Why were the Imperial soldiers, who should have been hiding in the back room, behind her? Grugell couldn't even turn around to face her unbelievable reality.

"We weren't hiding in the back room. We were two doors up."

"What did you say...?"

CHAPTER 3

"You've underestimated what an Imperial commander can do. Our boss is a slacker and a fool, but she's not dumb."

It had been what Mismis had said.

"Jhin, over here! No one's in this room in the very back!"

She had told them to hide in the back room, yelled, in fact, to make sure the witch heard the sham on purpose.

"B-but the footprints!"

"We backtracked. We left footprints in the snow all the way to the back room; then we walked in *the same footsteps back to where we came from.*"

"Impossible!"

That was a method of escape used in the animal kingdom. Tundra hares would do that on instinct to evade foxes. The wisdom of the meek trying to survive had gotten the better of the witch.

"Don't underestimate Imperial soldiers, Grandma."

"—You scum!"

"Lights out." Jhin hit her in the back of the head with the muzzle of his handgun. He didn't let her use her astral power, knocking the witch unconscious. She crumpled onto the carpet of snow.

"…A-are we going to be okay?" Sisbell peeked out from the room, looking down at the unconscious old woman before sighing with relief. "Th-this is no time to be relieved," she said to herself. "We must not have seen other assassins because they withdrew, so they wouldn't get caught up in Grugell's astral power. We need to run while they're making themselves scarce…but I worry about leaving her here."

"We need to leave her be." Mismis looked down at the collapsed woman, not missing a beat as she shook her head. "We already decided to escape from this place. I'd like to use her as a hostage, but we're not in a state where one of us can carry her on our backs *and* run."

"I—I understand. In that case, let's head downstairs. We may be able to leap outside from a servant's room!" Sisbell pointed at the stairs.

In that instant…the ultimate cannon blasted. Magic Shot of Corpses.

The laughter of a witch echoed from out of nowhere. No one understood what it was.

The first floor of the old castle had been blown away.

Sisbell, the three members of Unit 907, and even the armed soldiers attacking the villa were knocked unconscious by the force.

Was it two seconds? Or more than ten?

They couldn't tell how much time had passed.

The old castle leaned without a ground floor. When Mismis opened her eyes, not quite conscious, the whole place was dark.

"………Huh?" She was on her side, collapsed.

The passageway was lurching over.

It seemed the electrical lines had been severed. The lights were all off. She could tell from the moonlight through the windows that tiles had fallen from the ceiling and that the vases and portraits hanging from the walls had tumbled across the carpet.

"Wh…what…what happened…?" She got up from the slanted ground, cautious. "Jh-Jhin? Nene? Where are you?"

She sensed movement.

It was Jhin, the silver-haired sniper, walking toward her and clutching his side. Behind him, Nene appeared from the darkness. It seemed she had sliced her lip open when she'd taken the hit.

CHAPTER 3

"Hey, boss. I said we're heading down to the second floor, not that we were going to blow the castle away."

"It wasn't me!"

"I know. It has to be the Hydra, but…what's going on here? That wasn't gunfire from a random soldier. Were they planning on leveling the place?" Jhin scanned the darkness several times. "Where's the girl we were guarding?"

"Huh?! Oh, r-right… Where's Sisbell?!" Mismis cried out.

They didn't see her anywhere. Though a witch, she was daintier than the rest of them. She must have been blown away by the impact.

"Found youuu."

A witch's beguiling laughter peeled through the lit passageway. Violet flames sparked.

The astral light quivered like a will-o'-the-wisp and illuminated what appeared to be a genuine monster.

"Found youuu, little Sisbell. Oh, not moving, are we? I see. You've fainted. What a relief. I was so worried I'd overdone it."

The monster picked up the unconscious girl and hoisted her over its shoulder.

The witch in violet. Vichyssoise—it was unmistakably her.

Her hair was flaming red and solidified like a gem. All her muscles had transmuted into something that looked like glass. They could see the windows and ceiling behind her body, transparent like a jellyfish.

Why was the monster that Iska had fought *here*?

"Wh-why…?!"

"Hmm? Oh, so there were still Imperial subjects around.

Which means Aunt Grugell must have lost. Not that I care." The witch carrying Sisbell turned toward them.

She had finally noticed Unit 907. Or that's what it sounded like.

"You really think I can be confined? Not a chance. The handcuffs to contain astral power are made from steel. To contain me, they need to find the real stuff forged by the Astrals."

It was like a *nightmare had resurfaced*.

Even Grugell, the Witch of the Midnight Sun, who they had been fighting against desperately until now was outshone by this *true* witch.

That was because she was an inhuman monster.

"I've got Sisbell under my supervision. Wonder what I'll do with you. Maybe I'll roast you up along with this villa."

"Th-then come at us. Give Sisbell back!"

"Well, that was what I'd been thinking, but I'm in a great mood right now. I just got my revenge, after all. It'd be a waste of time fighting you, so I suppose I could leave you be."

"...'Revenge'?" Jhin repeated back. "You can't mean..."

"The former Saint Disciple Iska, was it? I blasted him away just earlier—along with the whole first floor." She pointed her thumb down at the ground. "The ground on the third floor is even starting to lean over. This place should be collapsing in, say, oh, a couple minutes or so."

"No!" Nene howled, shoulders quivering.

"Iska would never—" Nene's yell echoed in the dimly lit corridor.

"Lady Sisbell?!"

Several footsteps boomed in the corridor. Three young girls who had been hiding in the back seemed to have heard the sound, each wearing a servant's uniform.

CHAPTER 3

"Ah yes, the servants of this place."

"Eek?!"

Once they saw the monster in front of them, they yelped. Fear, however, lasted only for a moment. They saw Sisbell on Vichyssoise's shoulder. Anger flashed in their eyes as they gritted their back teeth.

"Lady Sisbell!"

"Scoundrel! She's one of the most important people in the Sovereignty. Unhand her!"

"That won't be happening." The witch sneered. "She's not returning to you—ever."

"Silence!" One of the girls was indignant as she pulled out a self-defense knife. "Let go of Lady Sisbell, monster!"

"Stop! Don't be stupid!" Jhin didn't hold her back fast enough.

Not one of the servants of the villa had astral powers that could be used for battle. There was no way they could fight against a witch.

Especially not with a single knife.

"Ouch. Just kidding."

The blade stuck out of the witch's side, but all it had done was open up a small hole in her semitransparent flesh. Not a single drop of blood flowed from the wound.

"You can't beat me with that."

"Are you a monster?!"

"If you're violent, you're going to get roughed up yourself—and it's going to hurt. Like this."

"Uh...gah!"

Knife still sticking out of her side, the witch grabbed the girl's neck and slowly squeezed, staring into the servant's eyes. "Cute face. Cute enough that you were picked to work for the Lou. You probably haven't had a worry on your mind since the day you were born."

"Ah..."

"Maybe I'll burn that pretty little face of yours so bad that it'll never return to its original state. You'll never be able to get yourself to look into a mirror again."

"Uhhh?! St...stop..."

"Nuh-uh. I'm not going to be nice to you anymor—"

"Vichyssoise."

The witch's smile froze over.

She forgot she was even holding the servant as she turned and looked. Standing there was a black-haired boy, covered head to toe in dust. There were only faint scrapes on his cheek and forehead.

"You again?"

"...Now you've really done it. I almost died *again*." Iska held his astral swords. The white sword could release the astral power sealed away by the black counterpart just once.

If he hadn't had Talisman's astral power at his disposal, he would have been blown away with the first floor by the Magic Shot of Corpses.

He'd seen the astral power once before. His split-second reaction had made the difference between life and death.

"How inhuman can you be?!" Iska cried out.

The witch was quick to make a judgment call. After fighting him once, she knew it in her bones—fighting this Imperial swordsman was dangerous.

"Let go of Sisbell!"

"You were seven seconds too late, intrepid knight." The witch hurled the servant at Iska. She hadn't just tossed the servant; she'd basically launched the girl like a human cannonball.

"Guh?"

CHAPTER 3

"Ah-ha-ha-ha! Too bad I couldn't off you. But it's over now."

Iska caught the girl. In those few seconds, the witch leaped out of the window with Sisbell over her shoulder. She used gravity to levitate in midair. Even Iska could no longer go after her.

"This place was destroyed *by the Imperial soldiers*. Several hundred citizens have already witnessed it. You have no place to run."

"Vichyssoise!"

"Good-bye, Saint Disciple. I'd be pleased if you were buried with the castle's wreckage."

The ceiling began to creak. After being on the receiving end of the Magic Shot of Corpses, the building itself was leaning to one side.

"Lady Sisbell!"

"Stop." Iska grabbed the hand of one of the servants who had run to the window. "You won't make it in time. You need to focus on saving your own life."

"Let go of me… What do you know? She's important to the Lou family. What good are we as servants if we can't even protect Lady Sisbell?!"

"We'll go save her," Iska said.

"What?" Her mouth hung open, her eyes wide.

What nonsense was this Imperial subject spouting? The two behind him suddenly lost the ability to speak.

"We'll save her. We'll go rescue her right now, so get out of this place and hide in a safe location."

"…What are you…? Keep dreaming, soldier…" The girl didn't stop trying to shake Iska off as he held onto her hand. "What can you do? You want us to trust you?! Lady Sisbell was kidnapped right in front of our eyes! And you just watched!"

"You let yourself get taken hostage," Jhin chimed in.

"Uh!"

His comment stopped the girl in her tracks.

"Why do you think Iska called out that witch's name to distract her? If he hadn't, you would've been roasted by that monster, and your life would've been over."

"......Th-that's..."

"If you hadn't been taken hostage, there was a fifty-fifty chance that we could've gotten Sisbell back. Those chances nose-dived when you let yourself get hotheaded."

That was why Jhin had tried to stop her at the beginning.

"*Stop!*" Jhin had said.

Iska had been trying to get behind the witch. Jhin had meant, *Don't get in the way*, but none of the servants had realized that.

"We'll try again. We'll get Sisbell back—for sure."

The knife that had pierced Vichyssoise was on the floor. Iska picked the blade up and pressed it into the girl's palm, wrapping her fingers around it.

"And if I can't do it, you can take my life yourself. You can take it out on me with this knife."

"What?!"

"We can't tell you why, but we'll risk our lives to protect Sisbell, at the very minimum. We came into this enemy nation planning to obey the laws. If you want to protect her, then follow our directions for once."

"......"

"You two."

The two girls holding lights suddenly snapped to their senses and looked up when Iska called to them.

"Where are the others? If they're still hiding, you need to get them right away. This place is going to collapse."

"Uh, um, well..."

"Hurry!"

CHAPTER 3

"Y-yes, sir!" The two girls scampered farther into the castle.

Yumilecia, Ashe, Noel, Sistia, and Nami—the five servants working at the castle. If they were evacuating, they needed to go together.

...*If they don't make it, I wouldn't be able to face them.*

...*Not Sisbell. Not Alice.*

"If you promise to listen to us, I'll let go of your hand."

"Okay..." Yumilecia, the oldest girl, gripped the knife with her now free hand, quietly sheathed her blade, and bit her trembling lip. "We'll listen to you but only for tonight, if that means getting Lady Sisbell back..."

2

The palace.

Gunshots in the night. Screams ringing from the grounds. These sounds clung to the ears like the damnations of the dead.

...*I'm going to lose my mind.*

...*I'd rather be on the front lines of the battlefield than at the castle in this purgatory.*

"This is serious!" Alice's skirt billowed as she continued to sprint through the plaza.

The soldiers screamed. She couldn't tell if they were coming from the astral corps or Imperial forces anymore. All she could do was try to pacify the hellfire's sputtering embers.

"Where are the firefighters?! What happened to the fuel tanks?!"

"Th-they're still on fire! Imperial soldiers are staked out near them. We're already at capacity trying to evade the snipers and attempting to contain the fire!"

"...So they're not attacking and devoting themselves to keeping the fire going."

All the Imperial army had to do was let the flames grow on their own.

Then I'll go—Alice stopped herself from saying that out loud.

At that moment, Rin was evacuating the wounded to the underground shelters.

...Rin! What are you doing? It's been twenty minutes.

...You promised to meet me here.

She hoped Rin was just busy. The worst-case scenario would be if she were stuck in place because the Imperial army was attacking her.

Should she wait? Or should she go in search of Rin?

Every ten seconds felt like a minute. As she gritted her teeth and stood firm, an earth golem hurtled toward her. "Lady Alice!"

"Rin?! I'm glad you're safe. Are the wounded okay?!"

"It took me time to get in touch with the medics, but they're all in the Lou's shelter and receiving treatment." Rin leaped off the golem. "The House of Hydra have come with their medics and guards arranged by *Lord Talisman*."

"He just knows how to handle things. He's been such a big help."

"......"

"What's wrong, Rin?"

Rin made a face. "I saw what Vichyssoise looked like when she attacked Lady Sisbell."

"...Yes, I know."

Vichyssoise—envoy of the Hydra—had attacked Alice's sister, transforming into a bizarre monster. Alice hadn't seen what she looked like, but Rin had witnessed it, along with Sisbell.

Her crimes had been committed independently of the House

CHAPTER 3

of Hydra, according to the head of household, Talisman, but they had no way of knowing if that was true. Regardless, Sisbell could bring everything to light with Illumination once she was back.

"Lady Alice! I have an urgent request!"

It was one of Elletear's guards, an armed one who never left her sister's door, running toward them, illuminated by a light.

"An assassin! In the Queen's Space!"

"...What did you say?!" Her voice nearly caught in her throat. Alice and Rin looked at each other.

"Rin."

"I—I didn't hear about that, either. The Queen's Palace is guarded against invaders."

"It's a Saint Disciple!" The guard ignored Rin. "We discovered her two guards collapsed, away from the Queen's Space—both gravely wounded. The medics are doing all they can to stop the bleeding."

"A Saint Disciple..." Alice repeated those words again, turning them over in her mouth.

Iska's face flashed in the back of her mind. Then Nameless, the assassin dressed in active camouflage.

"So you're telling me to go to the queen immediately?"

"Y-yes. I am requesting that you check on her, but I am also worried about the eldest princess."

"In what way?"

"...Sh-she dashed out of the Star Spire and *headed straight to the Queen's Space.*"

Alice went pale. Rin doubted her ears when she realized what that meant.

"What?! My sister Elletear *can't fight!*"

"She was so worried about the queen that she couldn't stay put. She broke past her guards, though we tried to stop her, and..."

That was reckless.

Alice understood her concern, but it was rash of her defenseless sister to charge into a room with an assassin.

...She'll only make the situation worse if she's taken hostage.

...Why would you do that? You have to realize what will happen!

Alice couldn't comprehend this. Wouldn't those actions just cause more chaos?

"Lady Alice, please stop the eldest princess."

"Okay. You stay at the Star Spire. I'll go to the Queen's Palace. Rin," Alice called out. She leaped onto the golem's shoulder, stepping on its hand. The earth golem stood up without even waiting seconds, the ground around it rumbling as if it were a tank as it started to run.

"I'll go as fast as I can," Rin said. "If you talk while you're aboard, you might bite your tongue off, so be careful."

"As if I'd let that happen."

They looked farther into the grounds from the golem's shoulder. Looking up at the Queen's Palace gleaming like a dream from astral light, Alice tightened her hand into a fist.

"Why would you do such a thing, dear sister...?!"

About thirty minutes ago...

In the Star Spire. The eldest princess's chambers, the Small Room of Mirrors.

By the window of a sprawling room that looked like a suite straight out of a luxury hotel...

"You're such a good little girl, Alice."

Watching the lawns burn below, Elletear was rapt with the

CHAPTER 3

sight, eyes narrowing. Her little sister was putting a Herculean effort into extinguishing those flames.

"If those flames grow, there will be victims even beyond the palace. You're desperate to prevent that. What a wonderful desire to have."

She wasn't being sarcastic. Elletear might have wanted paradise to fall, but she wasn't so heartless as to wish for more victims. The fall of the Sovereignty was an entirely different matter from the sacrifice of its people.

"But it seems the Hydra don't share my sentiments."

"Hmm?"

"When you attacked my sister in the eighth state, you rampaged in the streets, apparently destroying buildings in your way."

"That's 'cause she had guards. Bring up your grievances to the Saint Disciple Iska, if you wanna blame someone."

In the living room behind Elletear, a redhead in prison clothes lounged on a sofa. A pair of handcuffs with a broken chain hung off her wrists.

"It'd be nice if you could at least tell me that I did a good job breaking out of prison."

"Wouldn't that be condescending? Breaking out of prison wouldn't be much of a job for you, Vichyssoise." Elletear snickered as she faced the window. "I envy your powers. If I had them, I wouldn't be frightened of anything."

"...That's something coming from you—considering you're *a monster*." Vichyssoise sighed from the sofa. "With your beautiful face and body, you could startle the goddess of beauty. But you've sure got some strange interests. Why are you sacrificing everything to get in with some beasts?"

"Who can say?"

"Not chosen by the stars, the princess casts aside her position to seek revenge on the planet and turn into a witch. Is that what you'd call a tragedy?"

"......" Elletear didn't respond at first. "Isn't it about time?"

"Oh, okay. Well, guess I'm off to capture Sisbell."

The red-haired witch stood up. Violet flames burst from her entire body, catching her prisoner's uniform on fire. It burned off her, and she turned from a person into a monster. She turned into something inhuman, something the Astrals had once called the Mutant Star in fear.

"I don't think there's much of a point having me go when Aunt Grugell is there."

"There's a Saint Disciple among them. Since he defeated you once, Lord Talisman would naturally be cautious."

"...You really gotta put salt in my wound? You talk to me that way, and your sister's—"

"Vichyssoise." The eldest princess kept her back turned.

The witch in violet shivered when she heard the princess.

"If you lay a hand on my sister, I will crush the Hydra immediately."

"...You plan on betraying my family?"

"I gave three conditions to Lord Talisman from the start. That was one of them. As long as you uphold those, we should be able to get along."

"......"

"Now off you go. I have an important role to play soon."

"Ha." The girl-turned-monster snorted. "Getting wounded hurts, even if you have a body like mine. I'm sure it'll hurt even more if it's a Saint Disciple doing it."

"I know."

"Hope you can keep it up. To dupe the whole world." She winked out of sight.

CHAPTER 3

Violet embers sprinkled to the carpet and eventually disappeared.

"……" Elletear did not turn around. The eldest princess, the daughter of the queen, observed the scene outside. "Alice."

She didn't care about the witch in violet. All she needed to see was her beloved little sister. Tonight would be the last time—the last time that she would be with her mother and two sisters.

"Your flaw is that you're too strong. I bet you think you can save everyone, even in this situation. You think you can fend off the Imperial army, save the queen, and be the hero. That's a splendid thing."

The middle princess, Aliceliese Lou Nebulis IX. It wasn't just her astral power that made her strong. It was her empathy and benevolence toward her people—and most importantly, her ability to be ruthless when she needed to be.

She could ignore her emotions. For the sake of protecting the Sovereignty, Aliceliese would fight the Imperial army in any merciless way—even as she cried as she did it.

She would stifle her feelings and weep through battle. She was that strong.

"But that won't do."

That wasn't enough. Alice wouldn't be able to make this place, the Sovereignty, a paradise for *all* astral mages in every sense of the word.

"Your ideals are founded on your own strength. Won't you only make this place a paradise for the fittest?"

What would happen to the underdogs who hadn't been born blessed with astral power? As the representative for all those people, Elletear would burn this faux paradise to the ground.

And to start…

"Let it burn into your retinas and feel despair, Alice—watch as the *Empire kills me*."

The eldest princess lightly caressed the windowpane and smirked.

3

The Nebulis palace. Moon Spire.

The battle between the Imperial forces and astral corps had blasted away the walls of the Moon Diadem. Wind blew into the upper levels. Deep purple solidifications of astral energy crawled out of the floor, destroying it in the process.

"Are these Grandfather Growley's avatars?!" Kissing scowled.

The giant made from astral energy looked out from the hole in the floor and reached up, trying to hoist itself from the lower levels. It was unharmed, even while touching the floating thorns. Kissing's powers could make anything disappear. In terms of destructive potential, she was the strongest in the Zoa, but Growley's avatars were unharmed by physical force.

"I love my grandfather, but I hate these..." Kissing pouted, agilely leaping away.

Her Thorns and his Vice were incompatible. Even Kissing could do nothing but keep her distance when the avatars did what they wanted to the place. She needed to keep herself from getting caught up in it.

On the other hand...the Imperial unit who Mei led didn't know what the avatars were.

"M-ma'am! Our guns don't work on them!"

"That's 'cause it's astral energy. These will be annoying to deal with."

Mei glared at the giants crawling up. The Ruined King Hurricane on her shoulder was in a state where she could fire it at any

CHAPTER 3

moment, but her instincts told her she needed to prioritize figuring out what the astral power was.

"Bullets go right through them and the little miss's thorns don't work on them. Which logically means it's pure astral energy that physical force won't work on…"

How had the avatars broken through the floor? If they didn't exist in the physical form, then they shouldn't have been able to destroy anything material.

"So what's going on, Names?"

"They're avatars created by the astral power of Vice or whatever. To put it bluntly, they're invincible, apparently."

The soldiers stepped back in surprise. Empty space blurred, and a man wearing a full body coat appeared out of thin air. The Saint Disciple of the eighth seat, Nameless…

"Where's your left arm?"

"You touch one of those things, and you'll end up like me. The heads of household are certainly something. He's tough to handle solo, even for a Saint Disciple."

"So you ran off?"

"I'll stop him next time."

"…Hmm, assuming there *is* a next time," Mei joked, then her expression dropped, eyes narrowing like a beast's.

Giant humanoid avatars crawled up to form a wall where the two Saint Disciples stood in the passageway. Cerberuses pounced from the hole.

"Just to confirm: Are you sure they're invincible? What if we used missiles or fire?"

"I doubt that would work. If anything, that would increase our sin count and make them larger. It defies logic. It's so inconvenient. But they don't distinguish between friend or foe."

The avatars had scrambled after Nameless.

To fulfill their mission, they had created a path of destruction, trampling indiscriminately in their pursuit of Nameless. That was why the astral corps wouldn't rush here without a plan.

"Don't get the wrong idea." Kissing leveled out her right hand, and thousands of dispersed thorns wiggled, marking their aim on Mei and Nameless. "I will not let my grandfather handle this. I will be the one to eliminate you."

"Ah-ha-ha. So the head of household has poked his nose in his granddaughter's business—all to protect her. Someone get me some tissues! Maybe you should go back to your room for bedtime."

"...I really don't like you." The black-haired witch pointed at Mei, who laughed. "Disappear—"

Jingle. It was soothing, seemingly unfitting for a battlefield that determined life and death. It came from none other than Kissing's ear. *"Kissing, return to the meeting point immediately."*

"Uncle On?!"

The communications device shaped like an earring was concealed under Kissing's hair. On and Kissing spoke in muted tones, but Mei and Nameless had superhuman hearing. They heard everything.

"Why?!" Kissing asked.

"Extenuating circumstances. I cut a fight short with a Saint Disciple. I'm heading there now." His voice sounded more aggravated. Kissing didn't even have time to pick up on that. *"Princess Elletear was killed in the Queen's Space."*

"...............Excuse me?" For the first time, the family weapon, Kissing, let out a cute voice fitting for a young girl.

An Imperial assailant attacking the queen would have been believable. But...why had the *eldest princess* been in the Queen's Space?

"I can't believe it. She can't fight. She'd never go outside in a situation like this..."

CHAPTER 3

"That's exactly right. I thought she would have been evacuated to the underground shelter. Elletear should have known to do that—as wise and helpless as she is in this situation."

It was a reckless stunt—as if she had gone out *to* be slain.

"……"

"I've also only been informed by Alice's subordinate. We need to confirm the report... To be frank, I don't know what's happened, either."

It was at this moment that the plot of a single witch, Elletear... had completely overturned the assumptions of the Zoa.

CHAPTER 4

The Unforgiven

The main doors of the Queen's Palace were shut.

These doors could only be opened and closed using astral power, and they could not be shut for some time after being unlatched. That meant it worked entirely in the Imperial forces' favor if they could get them open. It would let them stream in and invade.

"Rin, you know what to do: Go in through the hidden door in the back."

They ignored the main doors and headed to the rear. Alice ran along the backside of the sprawling castle where the light did not reach.

"Lady Alice, I understand why you're in a rush, but you must keep your wits."

"I'm perfectly calm."

An awkward lie.

She was panting. Sweat formed on her forehead, which was uncharacteristic for her. She knew she was far from acting the part of a composed princess. Her heart pounded out of her chest.

…An enemy is in the Queen's Palace. A Saint Disciple is too dangerous of an opponent.

...I hope Elletear and the queen are safe.

"Hide, Rin."

They concealed themselves in the shrubbery along the outer wall of the Queen's Palace. Nothing seemed to be there, at least through the eyes of the Imperial forces. Alice—a trained mage—could spot the faint presence of astral light on the wall.

"Astral powers, it's me. Listen." Alice held out her hand.

The wall seemed to squirm in response.

The Queen's Palace was alive. Reacting to a descendant of the Founder Nebulis, the microscopic powers came to life and created a small tunnel in the wall.

"I can't see Imperial forces. If we go now, I don't think they'll notice this door."

"Let's hurry, Rin."

They sprinted through the hidden tunnel into the first-floor hall of the Queen's Palace. There, they found the royal guards ordered by the queen and one of the Astrals.

"Lady Alice, you're back!"

"We have a report. Earlier, Lady Elletear—"

"I already know." She nodded at her subordinates and ran down the hall. "I'll go to the Queen's Space immediately. The three of you will come with me. The rest can continue to keep guard!"

...I wonder how long this feeling has been with me.

...When did I realize something was off about this fight? Something bothers me.

She felt something—something foreboding. She couldn't shut down this feeling of uneasiness in her mind. In the hundreds of battles that Queen Mirabella Lou Nebulis IIX had fought, instinct

CHAPTER 4

had led her to the right path every time. In Imperial minefields. In plains poisoned by gas. When her comms were intercepted. When dealing with spies. When they were surrounded.

Her sense of smell was picking up the scent of death.

"I wonder why I get that from you."

She wiped away the dust that had settled on her lips. The Queen's Space where the queen stood had been *leveled*. It was her rampaging. Round columns that supported the roof had been sliced into discs. Where there had once been stairs were now piles of stone cut like tiny dice.

Plink-plink. Stained glass crumbled from the shattered windows.

"A scythe made of air. It once even cut an Imperial bomber in half. I decided that using it on a person would be too inhumane and held back in the past, but I see no reason to have restraint for someone who's treacherous enough to try to kill the queen."

"……" The Imperial assailant sat slumped on the ground under the cracked wall. He held his sword, completely unmoving, as a small puddle of his blood formed under him.

"Tell me how this makes sense. Why are you still alive?"

"……"

"I can hear your heartbeat. The atmosphere picks up all sounds. Even the tiniest of breaths."

"I see. That's a useful power," observed the swordsman matter-of-factly. He shook off the blood that had gotten on his crimson hair. Part of his armor had been gashed wide open, but he stood up as if to show that didn't affect his battle readiness. "You're atrociously cruel—expected, I suppose, for the Founder's descendant. You can use your powers when attacked from behind. It has many applications."

"…Why are you still alive? It seems you won't answer my question."

"It's because *I'm me.*"

"......"

"You must think I'm spouting nonsense. I have no intention of forcing you to understand." He swung his sword, which was as long as he was tall, bringing it upright. The Saint Disciple of the first seat, Joheim, followed the queen's movements with his eyes. "This time, I'll kill you."

"You're right. I don't understand what you mean, and I don't like the way you're looking at me. I can tell from experience that it's not a good look."

She took a step back on the cracked floor. With liquid-smooth movements, the queen tapped the ground with her toe.

"So disappear. Vanish in the wind, your unmarked gravestone."

Under the impact of Divine Wind, Mandala, the walls of the Queen's Space buckled. Winds layered upon each other and begun to blow in the Queen's Space. The disarrayed gusts created a geometric barrier that twisted anything around it and annihilated its surroundings.

In normal circumstances, she would use this to lay siege. It was one of her secrets to destroying a walled city, fortress and all. Used on a small scale in the Queen's Space, this attack couldn't compare to the original in raw power.

"It looks like you did underestimate me," Joheim observed.

The man was unscathed. He had slipped past hundreds of violent whirlwinds. The greatest swordsman among Saint Disciples pursued her, coming right up in front of her eyes.

"What?!"

"Your winds *avoid astral energy* as they push forward."

It was a large-scale attack. That was why she'd contained herself from unleashing all of it.

They were in the Queen's Palace. Had her people run into the

CHAPTER 4

room now, they would have been pulled into the winds and torn from their limbs.

So she had curbed her astral power, making sure it wouldn't hurt astral mages.

"That was your downfall."

"Why...you don't mean?!" Alarm found its way into her voice.

The Saint Disciple of the first seat. Joheim. The assailant from the Empire.

This was his true identity.

"You were the traitor."

"That's right. I betrayed the queen to change the Sovereignty."

Joheim. He had been born in the Sovereignty, an astral mage who had betrayed paradise and gone to the Empire. The queen hadn't known that, which was why her inhibited attack, intending to not hurt any astral mages, had been fatal.

"I knew about you, but you, the queen, couldn't care less about me. I was just an enemy combatant to you. That's what made the difference."

"Grk?!"

A single long sword. In her heyday, she would have been able to leap away from it in an instant as the best war automaton of the Sovereignty.

Did I dodge it?

And then she saw her tattered royal dress sliced into ribbons. Blood sprayed. She was lucky that she was only cut from her left arm up to her shoulder...or perhaps not so lucky. The Saint Disciple was already preparing a second strike.

"This will change history."

The blade intending to destroy the paradise for astral mages came down. The queen could only accept that this was the moment when she would meet her doom.

"Mother!"

"................Huh?"

Someone was shouting.

The eldest princess, Elletear, had shielded the queen, wounded by the Saint Disciple's sword.

"...Mo...ther...run......" Her back still facing the queen, the eldest daughter fell to her knees.

The Saint Disciple was showered in the blood pumping from the wound from Elletear's shoulder to her chest. Before the queen, her mother, could see the scene through to the end...she fainted.

The queen was struggling to keep conscious due to the wound on her arm—and her mind had shut down upon seeing the tragedy that befell her daughter.

She lost consciousness.

The eldest princess was sliced open, drenched in blood.

The witnesses to the event were none other than the Saint Disciple Joheim and...

"...Elletear? ...Mother? ......"

The Saint Disciple turned around.

Far ahead of the swordsman who gripped the bloody long sword stood a girl in the doorway of the Queen's Space. A purebred wearing a white royal dress. A witch with beautiful golden hair.

"I don't know who you are, but it looks like you were too late," came the steely murmur of Joheim, the unforgiven. "This nation has fallen."

CHAPTER 5

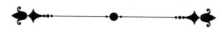

Aliceliese the Ice Calamity Witch

No scream came out of her.

Instead, what filled the Queen's Space was Elletear's blood from the wound that crossed chest to shoulder.

"...Mo...ther...run......"

As blood poured from her mouth, Elletear fell like a puppet with cut strings. Queen Mirabella collapsed behind her, and the two of them did not stir.

"...Elletear? ...Mother? ......"

It couldn't be real.

Alice doubted her own sanity at first. She'd never seen anything like this before, not even in her worst nightmares. In the Queen's Space, she bore witness to the tragedy of her beloved family dying.

"I don't know who you are, but it looks like you were too late. This nation has fallen."

The swordsman holding the bloodied sword turned to her. She didn't recognize him, but she knew he had to be the Imperial assailant. A Saint Disciple? Maybe. At the moment, that didn't matter. She knew one thing: This man had committed an unforgivable crime—and that she was saddled with regret.

She had been *naive*. That was why she hadn't been able to protect the queen or her sister.

It just proved her point. It proved the Empire needed to be destroyed.

"Guess you're next," the man said to her.

"How dare you, Imperiaaal subject!"

For the first time in her life, she growled, seeing red.

She knew her scream was unbecoming of a princess, but who would stop her?

...Until now, I've suspected my sister of being responsible for the coup d'état.

...I thought that was part of the reason why she'd taken Sisbell to the villa.

But it hadn't been. Her sister had been *innocent*. It was a misunderstanding that she couldn't take back.

After all...there was no way someone trying to *usurp* the queen would *protect* the queen. Her sister Elletear hadn't been the traitor in the House of Lou.

"—Imperial subject, I will never forgive you!"

She couldn't control her astral power. Its energy—pushing the limits of her full capacity—seeped from the crest on her back, turning into frost that manifested behind her like two blue wings.

"Frost, huh? So you must be the Ice Calamity Witch."

"That's right. To you, I'm a witch."

She pointed—right at the sword that had been brought down on her family. If it meant getting her revenge, she would become a witch to bring about the destruction of the Empire.

CHAPTER 5

"I'll freeze over Imperial cities. And you!"

Frost blasted toward him, materializing into ice blades that rained on the Saint Disciple. However...

"It seems you don't understand the situation." Joheim held a shield in his hand—a human shield. He held the eldest princess, who was bleeding freely from the wound across her chest.

"Lady Alice, don't do it!"

"...Guh?!"

Alice snapped back to her senses when Rin yelled at her. She stopped just as she had been about to attack. The ice in the air melted. If she hadn't stopped, her blades would have pierced through her sister, the hostage, instead of her intended target.

How dare he disgrace her sister. After all that she'd experienced, Elletear had been reduced to a human shield. This act of barbarity was beyond description.

"I've captured a purebred. I'm returning to my nation."

"Silence! ...I...will never forgive you. Don't you dare think you'll get back to the Empire in one piece!"

"We'll see about that." The swordsman changed direction, still holding her sister in the crook of his left arm. As soon as he turned his back on Alice, he started racing toward the back of the Queen's Space.

...Is he trying to escape?

...But it's just a wall over there. The only door is behind me.

No.

There was one other door, an emergency corridor known to only the royal family and those close to them. But it wouldn't open unless it were touched by a descendant of the Founder.

"I have the key."

That was Elletear in his arms. He took her unmoving hand and made her touch the wall. When the astral powers sensed the eldest princess of the House of Lou, the wall tunneled, making a passage.

"How could you use my sister like some tool?!"

"I'm making use of her full potential." Then he bolted from the Queen's Space.

The hidden passage was directly connected to the grounds. His plan was to meet with the other Imperial forces and take the eldest princess, Elletear, back to Imperial territory.

"Rin! How is the queen?!" She turned to her attendant.

Rin and the three guards accompanying her surrounded their collapsed queen. Two of them were already in the middle of requesting backup on their communications devices.

"She's alive. But the laceration on her left arm has gone to the bone... It's a miracle it's still attached." Rin bit her lip, next to her unconscious leader, who seemed to be in pain. The attendant had stopped the bleeding by tying a thin thread around the shoulder artery.

"She needs surgery for her arm ASAP. When the medics arrive, we'll need to take her to the medical room, and they'll need to start procedures immediately..."

"I trust you to handle it. Do anything as you see fit."

"...Lady Alice." Rin held her breath. "You're not going after him, are you?"

"No. I'm going to go after Elletear."

The priority was rescuing the eldest princess. Her secondary concern was tearing that man limb from limb and destroying the Empire.

"If anything happens, Rin, inform me immediately!"

Alice didn't even wait for a reply before she started running and slipped through the hidden door, out of the Queen's Palace.

"Where is he?! Where is that man...?"

CHAPTER 5

She was sure the Saint Disciple carrying her sister had been standing here just ten seconds ago. They couldn't have gone far. Under the faint light, Alice could only make out black stains on the pavement.

Elletear's blood.

Time was of the essence. Her sister's wound didn't compare to the queen's cut. If her sister didn't receive immediate medical attention, it would be a matter of life and death.

"I won't let you escape. I won't let you have your way with my sister…!"

The trail of blood led to the plaza on the grounds. Farther in, a plain parked car began to drive away.

"Are you trying to kidnap her?!"

So the Saint Disciple's aim hadn't been to meet with the Imperial army. He was going to immediately take the purebred back to the Empire.

Alice would never be able to reach them on her own legs. What could she do? Would she order the astral corps to pursue them and close the borders?

"Lady Alice, over here!"

A white government car screeched behind her. One of the royal guards from the Queen's Space was in the driver's seat.

"Lady Rin entrusted me with an order: to prepare a car to go after the Imperial forces who have taken Lady Elletear."

"An excellent decision. Floor it!"

Alice dove into the passenger's seat. Before she even had time to put on her seatbelt, the car began to accelerate in pursuit of the other vehicle, tailing it out of the palace grounds.

"Are they headed to the residences?"

"They must plan on getting on the highway. Central Interstate 8 is directly connected to the border." The guard who gripped the steering wheel held a communications device in his other hand.

"*Call to Checkpoint. Vehicle carrying royalty. Princess Elletear has been taken by the enemy, who is trying to get on the highway. Close off all borders.*"

They raced through the town in the middle of the night, the enemy vehicle ignoring traffic signals. They did the same.

Cars around them blared their horns, but they just didn't have time to mind the right of way.

"Hurry! My sister is on the cusp of death. We don't have enough time to chase them to the border. It'll mean her life!"

"I understand that, but—!"

They couldn't close the distance. In this high-speed car chase, only five seconds separated the two vehicles. They could *see* the car carrying Elletear, but they just couldn't seem to catch up.

…This is unbelievable. How can they drive so perfectly at this speed and time of night?!

…I imagined they would be spending all their energy just making sure they're on the right route.

She had to assume they were already familiar with the central state's roads. Without a shadow of a doubt, there was a traitor of the Sovereignty—and whoever it was had to be in that car.

"—There's something I need to say in advance," she voiced to the driver gripping the steering wheel next to her. "It's about what we'll do once we've caught them. If my sister is safe, we must immediately take her to the closest hospital."

"Of course."

"But…if she's not well…or if we're not fast enough rescuing her, I would like you to return to the royal palace right away."

"Y-yes, ma'am. To get back to the queen, you mean."

"No."

Her next words were going to be the most heartless statement she'd ever made in her life.

CHAPTER 5

"To crush the remaining Imperial army. Not a single one shall step foot in their homeland again."

"……"

"If my sister isn't safe, I don't know if I can keep my emotions in check. So I'm telling you in advance. I'm counting on you."

"…Understood."

Outside the window, the passing scenery changed from towering buildings in the inner city to the suburbs outside the city center. They headed onto roads that spread into the quaint countryside and woods.

"Lady Alice, the enemy vehicle has stopped… N-no, it hasn't!"

The vehicle *had* screeched to a stop.

But only for a moment. The car visible from their windshield started to reverse, racing at them.

"They couldn't possibly be—?!"

Before she could say anything else, Alice's vision was in flames. The car had exploded.

While astral power instantly activated its automatic defenses to human threats, it was slow to react to mechanical threats. The close proximity of the bomb had made it difficult for even Alice to respond appropriately.

…*So this was a trap.*

…*They made me think Elletear was being taken away, but the car was empty.*

She was starting to lose consciousness. Right as she felt the heat of the flames, the car holding Alice was blown into the air by the blast.

"—"

"Lady…Al…ice…please…keep it together…"

She opened her eyes. Alice felt the coolness of metal in the car that had been turned over on its side.

Astral power of steel. The guard had controlled metal and torn away part of the car to create a makeshift shield, protecting her from the direct fire of the blast.

He, however, had only managed to make *one* shield.

"What about you?!"

"I'm just happy...you...are...safe..." Turning his back to the windshield, the driver slumped onto Alice's lap. His uniform had burned off his back. His skin was red and angry.

"You protected me..."

She received no reply. After guarding her, he had lost consciousness.

"Please wake up. I'll get help right now!"

She placed her hand on his burned back, covering him in frost to tide him over. She got out through the car window and grabbed the man, pulling him with all her strength.

Then Alice yelled into her communications device: "Rin, please, I need you!" She didn't have time to wait for her response. "Please have a medic come here immediately. It's an emergency!"

"Lady Alice?! How is Lady Elletear?!"

"They got away. Even the enemy car was a trap. No time for that now. Please get a medic team here. I have someone who's wounded. He was burned...protecting me..."

"I'll arrange for it immediately!"

Rin didn't ask where Alice was. She could figure out where her location was through the device and the royal palace's communication center. As long as Alice didn't move, physicians would be on their way in a little more than ten minutes.

"...I'm counting on you." She hung up and lifted her head.

The car that had exploded in the middle of the road was roaring from the flames. The embers fluttered down on Alice's shoulders like snow.

CHAPTER 5

By her feet, the guard lie unconscious.

Behind her was the car crushed from the explosion.

"……"

With all that in front of her…

"—Why?!" Alice bit her lip—so hard it bled.

Was she feeling anger?

No. That didn't do her emotions justice. The queen, her sister, and now even one of her subordinates—people were going down right in front of her eyes, life leaving their bodies like water dribbling from her fingers.

"I was supposed to save them—the queen, my sister, this man! …Why won't anything go right?!"

Alice had been convinced that she had the power to change the war. As soon as she had arrived at the palace, she worked on containing the fires like her life depended on it. She had run to the Queen's Palace and come all the way out here to rescue her beloved sister.

And all of it had been in vain.

Why hadn't she been able to save anyone when it mattered to her most?

"……"

Her sister was on the verge of death after that Saint Disciple had maimed her. And the queen required surgery immediately. Even this man who she had laid on the roadway needed to be brought to a hospital. Otherwise, who knew what would become of him?

…*The Imperial forces—no, all Imperial subjects!*

…*If this was part of your plan, I'll never forgive you.*

"Prepare yourselves… I will have my revenge…" She balled her hand into a fist.

That was when she heard footsteps…and realized she sensed someone running down the roadway.

But who?

She looked up to find a black-haired boy standing there, panting.

A swordsman with a pair of swords—one black and one white.

"Alice?"

"………Is…ka…?"

Now, of all times. On the night when the relationship between the Empire and Sovereignty had reached rock bottom…

Iska the Successor of the Black Steel and Alice the Ice Calamity Witch had crossed paths.

The girl had been made acutely aware that every single Imperial soldier was an enemy without exception.

Her sister and mother had been hurt by an Imperial subject. She couldn't let a single one get away. No matter who they were.

"……"

"…Alice?" The boy held his breath as he looked at her.

He must have noticed something right away—the wrath on her face and the astral energy seeping from the crest on her back. Everything was just so different from normal.

…Yes. Yes, I suppose that's right.

…You would be able to tell, somehow or other. Alice observed the Imperial swordsman when she realized her eyes were tearing up.

"…Why do I have to see you now, of all times?" Her lips, split from tooth marks, trembled. Her voice was weak as a whimper. "We…can't…call each other rivals anymore. We can't have a simple relationship anymore…"

"Alice? What are you saying? You have to listen to me—there's something more important. It's about Sisbell; she's—"

CHAPTER 5

"I know I told you to *stay at the villa*," she interrupted him, refusing to take anything else for an answer.

As soon as she'd heard about the raid, she was sure she'd told him upon coming across him in the hall of the villa before rushing to the royal palace.

"I want to believe that this has nothing to do with you. So if you want to prove that's true, stay in the mansion."

"Alice? Wh-what are you talking—?"

"Do not go outside under any circumstances. If you show any sign of collusion with the Imperial army, I won't forgive you!"

She knew she had warned him.

He was the one who had broken his promise.

"Listen to me, Alice! Sisbell was kidnapped! Vichyssoise from the House of Hydra escaped from prison and destroyed the villa!"

"...Sisbell was kidnapped?"

"I'm following after them. And then I heard an explosion, so I came to the road."

Is that the truth? She scrunched her face to hold back those words she had almost uttered.

...We can't do this. I can't listen to you anymore.

...Even if I want to believe you. I can't because of my position.

The Imperial army were enemies. And she was the princess who would succeed the queen.

"You say my sister has been kidnapped? And you claim it was Vichyssoise behind it, not the Imperial army? What if *you* were the one who helped make it happen?"

"Alice! What's gotten into you?!"

"……"

It hurt to have Iska look at her this way.

She knew that she didn't want to say this, even if she'd been forced to spit it out. But she needed to destroy the Empire to protect the Sovereignty.

She couldn't pardon any Imperial subject, regardless of their identity.

"I don't believe you! I can't believe anything you say, Imperial citizen!"

"…What?"

"It's ridiculous for you to tell me to trust you! I…I saw my sister killed in front of my eyes. By a Saint Disciple—just like you!"

Her voice echoed between them, strained and grief-stricken.

She couldn't stop the tears from trailing down her cheeks.

"And it wasn't just my sister. The queen, too. There's no going back anymore. I can't forgive anyone who would hurt my family or my subordinates!"

She couldn't even wipe away her tears…because she didn't understand why she was crying.

…*Why…?*

…*Why am I crying? Why am I sad?*

Was it because her family had been hurt? Or because…?

"I am Aliceliese, middle princess of the Nebulis Sovereignty. I must bring down the Empire. Even if it means taking you down with it."

"…Alice." Iska remained confused. He looked at her directly.

But it was no use.

She couldn't stop it anymore.

"Why?! Why is this happening?! I…never wanted to fight you when we're like this!"

That was it.

CHAPTER 5

That's why I'm crying—the biggest reason that I have to shout out. I wanted to see you on a battlefield—on a special one just for the two of us. I wanted to forget about the strife between the Empire and the Sovereignty. I wanted to escape from the battle between blood among royalty.

—I cherished our crusade.

But the dream was over.

And in the worst way possible. It had devolved into a future fueled by antagonism.

"I..." Instead of wiping away her tears, Alice spread her arms. The astral power on her palms twinkled, creating icicles from the void. "Former Saint Disciple Iska, this is a declaration of war *on you*. Prepare yourself for battle."

"Alice?! This isn't the time for tha—"

"There's no going back anymore!" Her voice was hoarse.

Alice pointed at the Imperial swordsman in front of her.

"I never wanted to fight against you in this unstable state! I never wanted things to end this way...!"

At the moment, the curtain drew open on the second battle between Iska the Successor of the Black Steel and Alice the Ice Calamity Witch.

Bright-blue astral energy.

It split into thousands, then tens of thousands of particles, soaring into the air before winking out of sight. Few had witnessed that fantastical scene. The unarmed civilians had fled to the underground shelters. The only exception was...

"This intense spark of astral power. Wondered who it was. So it's the middle princess. Mira's daughter."

He was on a slight hill in the rural area.

As if receiving divine benediction of the heavens, the handsome man with white hair was bathed in the moonlight.

Salinger the transcendental sorcerer. The felon who infiltrated the palace to attack the former queen thirty years prior. Over fifty, he had the physique and face of a man in his early twenties. Far from reaching its decline, his muscular form had instead become even harder.

"......"

He was looking down at something several miles below the hill. Anyone else would need specialized binoculars to see the scene, but he had astral powers at his disposal that did the trick.

"And who is that but the Imperial swordsman himself...?"

He clucked his tongue quietly. Salinger had suffered a defeat to that opponent in the past.

"The battle's over, sorcerer."
"You're a beast hiding under a swordsman's skin!"

"Can't make any sense of it. Why is he still in the Sovereignty? More importantly..."

This boy had protected Aliceliese's attendant. Did that mean the Imperial swordsman was one of Aliceliese's henchmen? That was what Salinger had once suspected, but now...

"I see. What an unfortunate twist of fate." The white-haired sorcerer let out a sigh.

A battle was developing below. Alice's astral power was turning the roadway and fields around them bright blue, freezing them over.

CHAPTER 5

She was merciless. It was clear she wouldn't go easy on the soldier based on her attacks, but her face was the ghastliest thing there.

She gritted her teeth. Her eyes snapped open as she continued to attack the Imperial swordsman with her astral powers.

"Princess Aliceliese. You really are Mira's daughter. You must believe this was all some scheme planned by the Empire."

The transcendental sorcerer knew that the Imperial raid was actually a joint effort orchestrated by the House of Hydra.

...Thirty years ago.

From way back in the day, he had known about this...far before the two below him had been born.

"How ironic. Nothing changes on this planet. Mira, didn't I tell you? You're not fit to be queen."

They were too innocent—Queen Mirabella Lou Nebulis IIX...and her daughter Aliceliese. They weren't suited to being the Founder's descendants. They couldn't withstand a battle between blood. He had foreseen they would eventually become tragic heroines—just like this.

"......Fools."

In a rare moment, the white-haired Adonis voiced his anger at others.

"So you're going to repeat the same mistake from the past."

INTERMISSION

Our Last Battle or the
Night of Shed Tears

1

Thirty years and some months ago, Salinger had been her one and only challenger.

Standing in front of him with her arms spread open was a descendant of the Founder, a beautiful girl—the one he called Mira, his greatest archrival.

"Salinger, you're made of brawn. I suppose that's the reason you lack brains."

"……"

"Any normal person wouldn't come out of that looking the same. Not after a blast of my astral power."

In a giant meadow of a nature preserve, Salinger laid on his back, freely bleeding over the grass and being approached by a golden-haired girl. She held brutally large knives in each of her hands. Her shoulder-length hair fluttered in the wind. Her pace was as precise as an engine. As she walked, her eyes showed no emotion, like a machine.

"You're a felon who's stolen over a hundred astral powers in our Sovereignty. In fact, you're trying to steal mine, too. It would be most appropriate to execute you on the spot."

"......"

"But I got my adrenaline rush, so I guess I'll allow you to live. For as long as you're my sparring partner," she said as she licked a scrape on her shoulder in the place of disinfectant.

She was practically feral. Even her clothes weren't the usual attire for the astral corps but a top that only covered her chest. The smallest rectangle of fabric necessary to make a skirt was wrapped around her hips.

She started to tug off those things that barely served as clothes right in front of Salinger.

"I'm going to wash off all this sweat in the water back there. If I go back to the palace caked in blood and dirt, I'll worry the vassals. What about you? You seem like you don't like being dirty."

"...Who would...bathe...with you...?"

Before he even finished, knives almost grazed his face where he lay down, still immobile. Technically, they took a layer of his skin with them.

"Then you hold on to my knives for me. They're custom, you know."

She didn't have on a thread of clothing. Even with a man right in front of her.

Around fourteen or fifteen, she didn't seem to be embarrassed about showing off her beautiful skin in the slightest. She *also* wasn't elegant in the least.

Was she really part of the royal family? Was this the candidate to be the next queen?

INTERMISSION

Anyone would have doubted it. But if they witnessed her in battle, those doubts would have been dispelled in seconds.

After all, she was the strongest queen candidate in history—Mirabella Lou Nebulis IIX.

"Salinger, how could you just let me outmatch you?"

"Salinger, you are so rough with your astral power."

"Salinger, is that really the best sneak attack you could come up with?"

Mirabella met him not with pity but with disdain.

When he would collapse, a bloody mess, after fighting the princess known as the war automaton, she would fix a cold glare on her sparring partner.

Then one day, she changed entirely.

The Nebulis Sovereignty. Central state.

Salinger could steal astral powers. Famously wanted for his abilities, he had been wandering around town incognito and bought his food at a bulk food store. He was on the way back to his base of operations.

He was pondering how he would next challenge his opponent.

"Oh..."

Midday at the intersection...a girl stopped in her tracks.

"Salinger?"

"...You're—!"

While Salinger loitered about town, Princess Mirabella saw through his disguise as she walked around in her own camouflage.

"I never thought we'd meet in a place like this..."

He hadn't healed yet. But what did that matter? The battle would begin as soon as they crossed paths. That was the tacit agreement between them.

At least...that was *supposed* to be the understanding.

"Ah...ah-ha-ah-ha-ha-ha-ha-ha-ha-ha-ha!"

He couldn't have imagined that his archrival would start to laugh out loud, clutching her stomach and doubling over.

"Ah-ha-ha-ha-ha-ha! Wh-what are you doing, Salinger? W-were...you planning on making me laugh to death?! Ah-ha-ha-ha-ha-ha!"

"...What did you say to me?"

"I—I mean, you—*the* Salinger—are walking around carrying a shopping bag from the grocery store! To think you were blending in with the normal people, checking out vegetables and meats and lining up at the register!"

"......"

Now that she'd said it...Salinger remembered that he was, in fact, holding grocery bags in both his hands.

"Just imagining the same haughty man who has the gall to tell me, *Mira, today is the day I'll make you kneel before me*, lining up with housewives at the grocery store register... Ah-ha-ah-ha-ha-ha-ha-ha-ha-ha! I can't take it! You win!"

She couldn't contain herself, throwing her body down to roll around on the ground. She didn't care that she was in the middle of an intersection in broad daylight or that the people walking by were all staring.

"Wh-what a frightening scheme! I can't believe it—you've incapacitated me!"

"...Mira."

"And you've even got a bargain sticker on your pack of meat! I presume you must have had a heroic match against those housewives for it!"

"Shut up!"

INTERMISSION

Tears had formed in her eyes after she'd noticed the bargain-price sticker through the translucent grocery bag.

Incidentally, the sticker had been a coincidence. Salinger hadn't put much thought into it when he had picked the thing up. It had just so happened to have the unfortunate fate of being a bargain item.

"...Tsk." He started to walk away. He'd lost the will to fight with the girl rolling on the ground, laughing.

Plus, attracting this many eyes was sure to bring the military police.

"Oh, please wait." Following him from behind was none other than the girl herself. "I suppose these sorts of serendipitous things happen. So do we have a truce today?"

"Zip it. Consider your life spared," he spat.

"Okay. I was so close to dying of laughter."

"......"

"Hey, wait! Could you keep it a secret from the royal family that I was hanging about in town?"

"...What?"

He'd never intended to tell anyone in the first place. If he even approached the royal palace, the astral corps would have pointed their guns at him.

"I got in trouble with a secretary for falling asleep during a meeting. I was so upset I stormed out of the palace. That's kind of my MO, I guess."

"...You did?" He looked hard at the girl who was more than half a head shorter than him.

"A conference is a place *designed* to take naps. My duty is to fight, so I need to get some shut-eye during meetings to recover my strength after going to the battlefield."

This was unexpected.

He saw her as a bloodstained war automaton and thought of her as the ghastly berserker on the battlefront. He had assumed she would perfectly perform her duties as princess. Precise like a machine. Indifferent like one, too.

But she was falling asleep during meetings? And she'd sulked and ran off after getting scolded by her retainers?

"It's like you're human."

"I don't understand what you're saying, but I'm counting on you to keep this secret."

Then she left. Her footsteps were silent as usual. There was no one who would have been as quick to turn their back on him than her.

"...A war automaton can *laugh*?"

It had been his first time seeing her do that.

The girl wouldn't let so much as an eyebrow twitch when she was showered in Salinger's blood. Just now, however, she'd been laughing so much that her face had crumpled. And most of all... she had looked cute while doing it.

He had thought her face was rather proportionate but like a pretty doll. He hadn't sensed any *human* charm from her before.

"Tsk." He clucked his tongue again and hurried along.

He'd been captivated by her. Salinger punched a wall in front of his eyes, as though that would change his reality.

"Only for today. Don't think I'll overlook you next time."

2

This was supposed to be a duel of life and death.

Salinger would challenge Mira to steal her astral power, and

INTERMISSION

she would drive him back. Even after they had met in the streets, that had not changed.

So since when had things become different?

When had he started to treasure these moments they fought? When had he started to genuinely wish this relationship would continue forever?

Everything changed thirty years ago, during the attempt to kill Nebulis VII.

Salinger had found himself involved in a peculiar plot. While in pursuit of the culprit involved in the scheme, he'd heard of the plan for a coup d'état against the queen.

But there were two targets.

"So you're telling me they're after the queen and…the candidate with the highest chance of winning the conclave, Mirabella…?"

Someone was after Princess Mira's life.

And that someone was another descendant of the Founder.

"…A battle between blood. Pathetic, all of you. Who gave you permission to *lay a hand on my girl?!*"

Guided by an unfamiliar emotion, Salinger headed straight to the Queen's Palace.

Mira was stronger than anyone he knew. All the Founder's descendants, however, were powerful beyond compare, and any plots involving a coup d'état would be on a massive scale. If they launched a surprise attack, even Mira would be in danger.

—*Someone…*

—*Someone needs to fight by her side.*

"Don't get the wrong idea, Mira. It's not because I feel sorry for you. I'm doing this for myself."

That was what he told himself.

And when he sneaked into the Queen's Palace, Salinger witnessed something…

*　*　*

Queen Nebulis VII had collapsed onto the ground.

"...No."

He'd been too late. Someone had caught onto the details of the coup...and the mastermind had rushed forward with their plan.

Salinger had been slightly too late. And that was when he saw the monster that had attacked the queen.

"What is that beast?!"

It was someone from one of the royal bloodlines—the Hydra. He saw one of them transform into a monster right before his very eyes.

Test Subject F.

A mutant witch had started attacking him, emanating a force that he couldn't describe. Their fight lasted minutes, but each second felt like an hour as he faced the hardest struggle for his life.

"Salinger?!"

When the mutant witch had escaped his clutches, all who were left in the room were the queen and Salinger...and Mira, who had come running to the scene.

"Her Majesty..."

The queen, collapsed, and Salinger.

Based on what she was seeing, Mira could only assume he'd *sneaked into the palace to steal astral power from the queen.*

"Salingeeer!"

For the first time in her life, she growled at him. The princess, a warring automaton, was experiencing the new sensation of pure, unbridled rage.

"...Did *you* attack the queen?!"

"......"

"Answer me!"

INTERMISSION

Had Salinger told her the truth, history would have changed course.

But he hadn't been able to. He was too proud to tell her and immolate himself by begging for forgiveness.

Please believe me. He couldn't imagine allowing himself to be so disgraceful as to offer her an explanation.

Mirabella could not believe him when he continued to be silent—because of her position and dignity as a princess.

Dividing the two were status and morals.

That was where they bid each other farewell.

She broke down in sobs. As she cried, she pulled out a blade and pounced on him.

"Salinger! Why would you do such a thing?! What compelled you to do this?!"

"...Mira."

"I thought of you as my archrival—my only one. I enjoyed being with you, even as adversaries. I wanted to spend more time with you. Why would you defile our time together?!"

They were no longer rivals. Salinger was a felon for hurting the queen, and Mirabella was the judge and executioner. Their relationship had devolved into one of good versus evil.

"...I never wanted to fight against you in this state of emotional chaos!"

At the end of their battle, Salinger was captured and sent to Orelgan prison spire in the thirteenth state. He was charged as the fiendish sorcerer who had invaded the royal palace to steal the queen's astral power.

He didn't intend to tell her the truth. He had never meant to get involved in the royal family's squabbles in the first place.

Salinger didn't care whether the current administration went down and ended up in the hands of the Hydra.

He only cared about her. And he had lost her trust. That was all there had been to it.

The leading actor of the past—Salinger—silently watched the scene unfold below him...as Iska the Successor of the Black Steel and Alice the Ice Calamity Witch approached the same fate.

CHAPTER 6

Our Twisted Battle or the Night of Promised Vows

When and why had our wheels of fate gone off its tracks?

Even as enemies, I'd always thought we had a mutual understanding that transcended our places in society.

In fact, I still think that's true.

That was why I scrambled after Vichyssoise to get Sisbell back from her captor.

"We'll save her. We'll go to her rescue right now, so get out of this place and hide in a safe location."

"Okay…"

"We'll listen to you but only for tonight, if that means getting Lady Sisbell back…"

The servants had fled the manor.

Commander Mismis, Jhin, and Nene were going to keep an eye on the crumbling estate while Iska pursued the witch on his own.

"Alice, listen to me!" Iska shouted, the air around them cold enough to chill him to the bone.

Astral power had covered the countryside and road with ice, smoothing over the land like a skating rink.

"I'm here because I want to save Sisbell. I'm not lying."

"I don't want to listen to what you have to say!" screamed the golden-haired girl, trying to contain a sob. "I...I saw my sister killed in front of my eyes. And Her Majesty!"

"...What did you say?"

"This is war. Of course, someone will be hurt. But as a princess, I need to get revenge for the royal family's suffering!"

She couldn't have an opinion on the matter. The middle princess Aliceliese couldn't have a discussion with an Imperial subject.

"The Imperial army have crossed a boundary they shouldn't have... Now, we really can't avoid war. Not until one of us has been burned to the ground!"

"......"

Everything had changed in minutes. Iska instinctively realized this when Alice had raised her voice. The relationship between the Empire and the Sovereignty was beyond rock bottom. It had returned to its roots.

Things had reverted back to a century ago...when the Founder Nebulis had started her rebellion. Even their personal relationship had regressed all the way back to when they had first met.

"You want us to fight until one of our countries is obliterated? Is that what you really want, Alice?"

"As a collective, yes. I don't get to call the shots here." The girl constructed a wall of ice between them, wiping away her tears. "My ultimate goal has always been to overthrow the Empire. But I never wanted to take things so far. I never wanted to think about eradicating the Empire or burning it to the ground... That would mean I stooped to the same level as the Zoa."

CHAPTER 6

Even if they could destroy the Empire in the war, it would come at the cost of casualties from the Nebulis Sovereignty—from royalty to the astral corps fighting in the trenches.

It, however, was too late to stop the wheels of fate.

"By meeting you, I learned that there are some sympathizers in the Empire. I wanted things to end as peacefully as possible when we overthrew the Empire, but the Imperial army ruined our chances at that future for all of us!"

The astral energy radiating from Alice almost bloomed off her body like a flower in the dark of night.

They were heading into the start of their final fight.

"Come at me, Iska, like you want to stop me! I won't be holding back, either!"

This was the second real battle between Iska the Successor of the Black Steel and Alice the Ice Calamity Witch.

Creak. Under Iska's feet, the ice rink started to crack.

It looked like something might be coming out of the fissures. Iska steeled himself. In front of his eyes soared a polished ice mirror that looked like an enormous jewel.

Eight mirrors surrounded him, towering over his frame.

"Ice mirrors?!"

"I'll say it again: I won't hold back!"

He'd never seen anything like this before.

…Ice is a pretty basic astral power, even if Alice's powers are on another level.

…They can deliver physical attacks or obstruct opponents. But this…seems different.

What were the mirrors for?

He couldn't imagine they would have special powers. At their core, the mirrors were just made from ice. If that was it, he assumed he would be able to break them using his astral swords.

"*Ice Calamity—Infinitesimal Fans of Light.*"

Lights flickered just for a moment. Iska was sure that it wasn't electric light as soon as he saw the mirrors reflecting at the edges of his vision. The light, faint and almost fantastical, started to converge.

Was the astral light thickening?

He recalled a conversation between Nene and Sisbell.

"*What is this energy...? It's not electricity—or gas. What's the source of this...?*"

"*It's light from astral energy!*"

The Object. A witch-hunting machine.

He remembered the signal that had informed them of when it would use its life-form integra.

"I get it now!"

The flash projected out of the eight mirrors—shooting not ice but the source of astral power—was astral energy. One ray of light would be reflected off a mirror, turning into two, and so on, amplifying power each time. Once they had amassed over a hundred lights, they shot through the target at the center—Iska.

Or rather, they should have.

Alice praised him. "Your instincts are ridiculously sharp as always."

It was her way of expressing her caution toward her incredible enemy.

"This is a new trick of mine," she admitted. "I'm still experimenting with it. I haven't even shown Rin yet."

CHAPTER 6

"...So I'm lucky." Iska leaped away nimbly, splatters of blood staining his cheeks.

In less than a second, he had escaped the eight reflective surfaces by an infinitesimal margin, jumping out of their range.

"If I'd tried breaking the mirrors, I wouldn't have made it in time."

"That's right. I thought you would try to break them right away, which is a trap."

"...It's almost like you came up with it specifically for me."

"I did. There's no point to using this on anyone else." Alice was looking straight at him through puffy, red eyes. "I've been preparing it ever since we first fought in the Nelka forest. But I stopped developing it before it was complete. I thought it was too unfair to use against you..."

She had been coming up with a strategy specifically to counter Iska. Any other Imperial soldier would have made a break for it as soon as they were surrounded by these ice mirrors.

But not Iska.

Alice knew he would try to push forward and use his skills to break the mirrors. She had been planning on using that against him by shooting him with light right as he approached the mirrors.

No swordsman would have been able to react to a shot of light.

...She's right.

...If she had perfected it, I would have been in trouble.

The flickering of the light had given him a sign of what was to come.

That was how Iska realized the mechanism behind her trick. If she would have seen it through to completion, there wouldn't have been a flicker to warn him.

"It's a trap, basically. It's not fair—and not even part of my original powers. I was hoping to rely solely on my own abilities when we settled things. But now we're in a situation where I can't say that anymore."

"...So you'll do whatever it takes."

"We don't have any time! The Imperial raid is still going on as we speak. I need to protect the Sovereignty!"

Toward an unforgivable enemy, she couldn't extend the mercy of considering whether something was fair or not. Alice wouldn't hesitate to use any tactic necessary, no matter how barbarous it might be.

To protect the royal family and her people...Aliceliese would stoop to any level and inflict anything she thought was necessary to secure her win. Even if it wasn't what she wanted herself.

"Attack me with all you have, Iska. Just like you did when we fought in the Nelka forest. I'll fight you like you're an Imperial soldier whose name I don't even know."

"You—" Iska gripped his swords.

He couldn't deny that she was emitting a murderous rage that seemed to freeze his skin. The person in front of him wasn't Alice but Aliceliese the Ice Calamity Witch, the greatest threat against the Imperial army.

...She's not kidding. And she wants to settle things when I'm supposed to be rescuing Sisbell.

...Alice wants to settle things here and now, of all places?!

A terrible twist of fate. The middle princess stood in his way, barricading him from saving the youngest princess.

"Move aside, Alice. I need to do something up ahead!"

"I'm telling you that you would need to kill me to pass! Kill me if you can!"

An ice golem formed beside Alice.

Was she creating more pawns for herself?

CHAPTER 6

Iska tried to figure out what exactly she was planning. The golem picked up the limp driver on the ground.

Alice's royal grab swished grandly as she stretched her arms out.

...She made a golem to protect her subordinate.

...Is she planning on freezing over everything around her at random?!

He narrowed it down to one possible technique, one astral attack, symbolic of the girl who went by the name of Ice Calamity Witch.

Great Ice Calamity.

The night air seemed to whistle, then screech. The countryside—the trees lining the road, the streetlamps, everything—was buried in surreal white mist.

This was *bad*.

Under the veil of night, the mist made visibility dangerously low. This was what Alice wanted. Iska might have been able to evade her once before, but now the night was on her side.

"Gah?!" Iska recklessly vaulted up, still unsure of how much of his surroundings had frozen over.

Crick. Something frosted over. A cold front of unprecedented size swept over him.

"......" Iska landed on top of an *ice* wall five yards up from the ground.

When he saw the scene again, it sent another shiver down his spine. It was like they were trapped in the Ice Age. The countryside, the streetlamps, the flipped-over car in the street—everything was frozen over. Had this been the battlefield, tanks and military bases would have become solid ice.

"I knew you would dodge it." Her voice came from behind him.

Beyond the wind sweeping up snowflakes stood a golden-haired girl illuminated by astral light.

"I honestly hadn't been that shaken up when you avoided it in the Nelka forest. In my mind somewhere, I assumed it had to have been a coincidence."

The girl stood on a hill of ice. White breath spilled out from between her glossy lips.

"So Rin was right in the end. She was always saying that the Imperial swordsman would inevitably become a threat to me someday. She told me that I shouldn't let you in."

"I could say the same about you. When it comes to being a threat, at least."

"......So..." Ice crystals were collecting on her shoulders. Standing at her full height, the Ice Calamity Witch continued, "Aren't you going to curse at me?"

"Hmm?"

"You can call me a witch. I am an enemy to the Imperial army, after all. And I declared war on you, too. So I would accept it if you wanted to call me a witch."

"......"

"It's fine. I won't mind if you call me tha—"

"Alice," Iska cut her off.

"Your voice is shaking. I don't want to hear you putting yourself down."

She opened her eyes wide. Her shoulders trembled slightly, and her lips quivered.

"—"

"This doesn't benefit anyone. I—"

"Stop!" She shook her head, disheveling her hair. Her voice

CHAPTER 6

was hoarse, almost like she would cough up blood. "Please...don't be kind to me. I don't have the right to be *your* rival any longer!"

The girl bit her lip, tears pooling in her eyes. They turned into glittering beads of ice like crystals in the shape of tears. The wind swept them away, but they kept falling, showing no signs of stopping.

"I need to be a princess of Nebulis! I need to destroy the Empire! So stop! Forget about everything, and fight me!" Alice screamed.

It was the saddest declaration of battle that Iska had heard from a witch.

"*Great Ice Calamity—Thorn Blizzard.*"

Ice daggers materialized from the wind in the space above Iska.

He'd seen her use this attack in the Nelka forest, but this situation was different. He had difficulty tracing the blades with his eyes in the middle of the night.

...It's no use. I knew I wouldn't be able to hold back.

...I'm fighting Alice, and she's serious about this!

He rebuked himself. If he didn't actually fight her, he would have no life left to live. His opponent was just that strong.

"Come, Iska!" Alice beckoned him.

So Iska threw himself at the blades that flew through the air.

They were coming at him from all directions—from above, of course, and behind, ahead, left, right, like a May shower. He didn't have the option of dodging this time.

All he could do was kill—before he was killed.

Alice had chosen this astral attack to corner Iska into making that decision.

"Hah!" Iska gripped his black astral sword and knocked away the blades coming at him.

He dove across the fissures forming on the surface of the ice, twisting his body around in midair like a cat. From the corner of his eyes, Iska watched blades graze his shirt cuffs as he just barely ducked.

"They're coming from below!"

He kicked and broke the needles of ice that formed below his feet.

Then he kept going forward. He didn't even pause to blink as he plowed toward the blizzard, like he was gliding over ice. He headed straight for the girl's bright-blue light.

"Now come, Iska. Let's end this here."

Aliceliese the Ice Calamity Witch thrust both of her hands out before her.

"No matter which of us wins, it'll be over now. We're going to end our battle—*aching from the regret that fate has made us settle things in a way we never wanted*!"

The wind whooshed past them, carrying ice and snow.

The cold front made by Princess Aliceliese blotted out their surroundings, bringing them back to the Ice Age.

"......"

The transcendental sorcerer Salinger, indifferent to the cold, watched the scene below from a low hill that overlooked the countryside. The man with white hair didn't flinch, even as the grass under his feet froze over.

"The fate of the stars. Is this what you wanted from the world?"

Princess Aliceliese and the Imperial swordsman were locked in battle.

The Imperial army and astral corps were still engaged in a

CHAPTER 6

fraught fight at the royal palace. In the background of war, Salinger was the only one watching the combat between the pair.

"...Or are you testing humanity? But there's no future beyond this futile fight."

Salinger didn't know the circumstances between the two, but he could guess what had happened. He'd seen this before. Alice had assumed the same expression as Mirabella had when she caught him in the Queen's Space thirty years ago.

"So the royal family will repeat the mistakes of the past..."

—Why do all our paths lead to outcomes that are so horrible?

She might have lamented the fate of the stars, bewildered by divine providence. But as a princess, she didn't have the luxury of hesitating. In past and present, the girls born to protect the Sovereignty had become playthings of fate.

"...I can't bear to watch this play out." Salinger turned his back on the fight below.

The fight would conclude in a few more minutes. He could tell from the gravity of their expressions. And it didn't matter to him who fell and who survived.

The one to survive this conflict wouldn't be the victor. They would have lost, too.

After all, there was nothing to be won from this battle. Waiting for them on the other side was pure emptiness. In other words, both fighters had lost the moment the battle had begun—lost to *fate*.

Just as the former princess and the transcendental sorcerer had thirty years ago.

"...I can't bear it," Salinger murmured to himself, irritated, turning his back on the pair as they headed to the final stage of their battle.

This was it.

Ice blades ripped through the night, raining to the ground, numbering nearly a thousand.

Iska, hounded by a shower of death, ran straight for the golden-haired girl.

"*Ice Flower!*" Alice thrust her hands in front of her.

The smooth surface below her feet cracked. A frozen shield bloomed like a germinating flower. This was a trait of her astral power—the ice flower—an invincible shield that could guard attacks launched by the Founder Nebulis.

Was this to counteract his astral swords? Iska tried to see if his guess was right.

Something protruded from the center of the flower.

A *seed*, beautiful and translucent like a crystal made of ice. Just large enough to hold in his hand, it started to glow from where it was enclosed by petals.

The light was coming from the center of the seed itself.

"Is this—?!"

"While this flower is activated, my astral power travels out of my body into the seed," Alice told him as she readied the shield with both hands. "This is my astral power itself."

"...That explains it."

The ice flower had fended off even Iska's swords in the past. His blade could cut through astral energy, but these petals were made from astral *power*.

CHAPTER 6

"I won't hide anything from you, since this is when everything ends...!"

Light burned in the seed. The output of astral power from the source itself was incomparable to the flash discharged from the eight mirrors.

The light surged.

Iska readied his sword, bringing it up at the same time that the light shot out of the ice flower. There wasn't a second, an instant, a moment of difference in timing.

The flash of light passed by Iska's side, shooting far behind him into the night.

......

............*Huh?*

It wasn't a direct shot. It hadn't even grazed his clothes. It was like its aim was screwed up. Maybe she had missed the first time on purpose? Maybe the next one would be the real shot?

He looked into Alice's eyes as she held her ice shield. That was when he noticed something. He realized why she had missed him.

Had she missed on purpose? No.

The Ice Calamity Witch had been trying to hit him. She had been meaning to shoot.

But she had missed.

"......"

"Wh-what's gotten into you, Iska?! Why have you stopped running?!" Alice, protected by the ice flower, screamed at him when she realized Iska had stopped in his tracks.

Iska was silent. He had halted right before his swords were within reaching distance of her.

He faced her.

"I-I'm going to shoot! If you don't put up resistance, then I'll—"

"It won't hit me."

"What?!"

"You can't see me clearly. Not when your eyes are *like that*."

The eyes of the Ice Calamity Witch...were flooded with tears. Her vision was blurry, and she could only make Iska out vaguely. At some point, her eyes had puffed up and turned red.

In the arctic blast, her tears had turned into little crystals, but she couldn't stop herself from crying. Tears trickled down her face from the corners of her eyes like a spring.

"......Uh... Aaah..."

The wind carried her sobs. The ice flower had come undone like an unraveling string. Her astral power had been depleted, returning to its owner's body.

"...Let's stop," Iska said, sheathing his pair of swords.

This was enough. This wasn't their crusade. They both knew that to be true.

"I'm going to say this clearly: I don't want to fight you when you've forgotten who you are, Alice. This isn't the time for us to engage in battle."

"...Ugh..." Her face turned stony. "I feel that way, too! But I already told you more than once: I can't forgive the Imperial army!"

"I think that's where you went wrong. It's not just the Empire scheming. The Founder's descendants took Sisbell and brought in the Imperial forces. And one of the descendants involved is your sister, the eldest princess."

"...My sister...?"

"That's what Sisbell told us—right after you left the villa."

As soon as Alice had left, the head of the Hydra had immediately launched an attack.

CHAPTER 6

* * *

"*I just…realized…*

"My sister Elletear is the traitor… I'm sure she's behind the scenes, trying to betray the queen!"

"Are you telling me you don't believe your sister, either?"

"It's not like that! I…can't believe *you*—I can't believe you when you say that Sisbell told you that!" Alice balled her hand into a fist. "I suspected my older sister was involved in the coup…but I saw Elletear about to die as she protected the queen!"

"That's suspicious because—"

"How can you doubt her after I saw her myself—?"

"*Listen to me!*"

"Eek?!" A yip escaped from Alice's lips.

This was the first time anyone had ever *berated* her.

She was speechless, scared of this unfamiliar sensation. There had never been a single person other than the queen who had ever scolded Princess Aliceliese. Even the queen would only give her a gentle warning.

So this was a first.

It was the first time Alice had experienced someone being angry at her.

"……"

"Listen, Alice."

She had the eyes of a scared girl as he addressed her.

"Your villa was destroyed by the Hydra. Even the people dressed as Imperial soldiers were their assassins operating under the orders of the head of household."

"…The head of household?"

"Talisman the Tyrant. He enhances his physical capabilities using the astral power of Waves. I'm sure of it."

"......" Alice's silence was her answer.

An Imperial subject knew about the powers of a purebred. This was one piece of proof that Talisman had attacked her villa.

"...Even I......" Alice broke her silence, letting out a tiny sigh. "Even I...don't think you're the type of person to lie. But..."

"But?"

"I can't decide these things on my own! I can't eliminate the possibility that you looked into Lord Talisman and his astral power before the Imperial forces started their raid. If I questioned Lord Talisman, I already know how he would reply!"

"The Imperial subject, Iska, has lied to you.

"My dear Alice. Are you really going to believe a fabricated story? Do you truly trust him over your own family?"

She didn't have proof to deny his claims.

The villa owned by the Lou had been essentially demolished.

Anything discovered under its debris would be products made in the Empire—guns, gear, and all. It would just lend strength to the idea that the Imperial army had attacked, not the Hydra.

...Of course that would happen.

...The only thing to prove the Lou family is under attack is Sisbell's Illumination.

That was why Sisbell had been targeted. Talisman had come to stop Iska himself. He had even used Vichyssoise to flatten the villa.

"...I...don't know what to do..." Tears started to form in Alice's eyes.

She didn't think Iska would lie, but she had seen for herself the amount of destruction and cruelty that the Imperial army could cause. She didn't know what was true.

CHAPTER 6

"Didn't Sisbell get kidnapped? I can't take the word of an Imperial subject who failed to protect her."

It was almost impossible to shake the general populace's absolute trust in the House of Hydra. Who would take an Imperial soldier's words as truth, especially when the queen had been maimed by his troops? Alice, too, had trouble trusting him.

"I...obviously don't want to fight you feeling this way! I wish I could come up with any excuse to keep from battling you. But there's nothing!" Alice wiped her eyes, drying the tears that blurred her vision, and looked at Iska through the arctic blast.

"...Huh?" Alice opened her mouth, dumbfounded. "Iska, is that—?!"

"Wh...what is this?" Iska noticed something when she pointed at his hand.

An infinitesimal bit of astral light around his wrist. It was so weak, and he had been so preoccupied with the situation that he'd failed to realize it.

...It has a gray light... That's not Alice's.
...Then who did this?

Was it a subspecies of astral power derived from curses?

Surprisingly, he felt no sense of malaise, though it was on his skin. If he had felt any pain, he would have taken notice of it even if he was distracted.

"It couldn't be..." Alice, still shell-shocked, staggered over to him. The light on Iska's shoulder reacted and turned into something like a butterfly.

A butterfly of light.

"I knew it! It's Affinity! It's Yumilecia... This is the astral power of one of the girls at the villa. Did you do something to her?"

"Me? I haven't done anything. The servants should be safe."

Yumilecia hadn't been hurt, even after being attacked by the witch. All five girls had evacuated from the old castle.

"That's not what I meant. Her astral power is used to deliver messages..."

"Huh?"

"She can touch a messenger to entrust her note with them. She must have touched you."

He could only think of one time—right before he had left the villa, when he had promised to rescue Sisbell.

"We'll try again. We'll get Sisbell back—for sure."

Iska picked the blade up and pressed it into the girl's palm, wrapping her fingers around it.

"If I can't do it, you can take my life yourself. You can take it out on me with this knife."

He had touched her hand. She must have covertly used her astral power on him.

"...Iska. I won't hurt you, I promise. Come closer."

He nodded silently.

Astral power had faded from Alice. It was her way of demonstrating that she wouldn't attack him if he approached her.

"Our attendants are no ordinary servants. The five of them can't fight, but they have astral powers to use in times of urgency."

"Is that what this Affinity stuff is?"

"That's right. It won't invoke unless it touches a specific person." Alice reached out her hand. Her fingertips were trembling, perhaps owing to an inner conflict that Iska couldn't possibly understand.

Alice touched the butterfly.

CHAPTER 6

* * *

"To Lady Alice, Lady Sisbell, Lady Elletear, or Her Majesty."

This was a message for her employers, which would play once when one of the four members of the Lou touched it.

"*I have a report. As one of your humble servants, I pledge to the royal family that these are my own words.*
"This Imperial raid was not just orchestrated by the Empire.
"The masterminds behind the coup are the Hydra."

Yumilecia hadn't been forced to say that by the Imperial army. If she had been threatened into making a statement, they would have used a tape recording. But she had exposed her own astral power to an Imperial soldier to leave this message.

This proved…the note was of her own volition.

"*The head of household attacked and demolished the estate with mages disguised as Imperial soldiers. I apologize for allowing Lady Sisbell to be taken. It was my fault.*
"The actual Imperial soldiers *saved us, concerned for Lady Sisbell's safety.*
"*Please have it in your heart to be accepting of the four of them…*"

A firsthand account from the Lou. It wouldn't hold up as evidence in an inquisition to pull Talisman from his position as head of the household.

However…for the princess, this testimony from her own servant was more than sufficient.

"……"

Upon carrying out its duty, the butterfly fluttered away, disappearing under the veil of night. Princess Aliceliese could only watch it go.

"......I see." The strength in Alice seemed to fade, even in her voice. "You were right...until the very end. I was the one tricked..."

It had all been a sham.

After the Hydra had ushered in the Imperial army, Iska and his companions had done everything they could to protect her dear sister. Alice should have directed her need for revenge at the Hydra.

The two hadn't had a reason to fight. Even if the Imperial forces attacking the palace were real soldiers, their plan wasn't associated with the boy in front of her. Alice finally was able to believe it all.

"I'm sorry! I'm so sorry...!" Alice crumpled onto smooth ice, sobbing.

Like a burst dam, her tears that had paused temporarily started to flow again. As she sobbed, gasping for air, her voice was so quiet that it almost disappeared.

"......I...just wanted to protect the Sovereignty and my family... Why did...I let myself do something so wretched to you...?" Alice wept.

She was defenseless. She couldn't see clearly through the tears.

If the boy was her enemy, he would have brought his sword down on the witch. It would have been simple. She would have just had to accept her fate.

"Stand up, Alice."

When Iska said her name, the princess's body jolted.

"There's something you've got to do before you go around apologizing to your enemies."

"...Huh?"

CHAPTER 6

"What are you going to do now that you know your sister's been kidnapped? Are you going to abandon her?" Iska asked the girl who looked up at him.

He just kept *talking* to her. "An Imperial subject doesn't care what happens to the Sovereignty or the queen. But I can't abandon Sisbell, and I'm planning on helping her."

"……"

"Are you just going to sit there? Because I'm going with or without you."

He wasn't saying niceties. He didn't even offer her a hand up. Their relationship *wasn't like that*.

"…You're ruthless." A self-deprecating smile flashed across Alice's face for a moment. Then she wiped away her tears with a fingertip and stood up on her own, staggering, but upholding her dignity as a princess. "Hello? A girl is crying in front of you, and you can't be bothered to say a single kind word or offer a helping hand? Imperial subjects are so barbaric."

"You can be disappointed in me, but—"

"*Thank you.*" Her breath brushed against his neck.

He had no idea what had happened. Before Iska could gather his thoughts, Alice's golden hair, soft as silk, tickled his nose. He felt the soft sensation of her chest against his.

"Thank you…for thinking of me as your rival again… If you're treating me the same, that means we can be equals, right?"

This wasn't a hug. She had just entrusted herself to him and wrapped her arms around his body.

Yes. There were no ulterior motives. She wasn't trying to get anything from him.

"…Alice?"

"—"

They only touched for a few seconds.

Before Iska could realize what was happening, the lovely witch princess parted from him and turned her eyes away.

Fate had changed course.

They weren't going to repeat the history between the leading actor and the princess—the destiny of Salinger and Mira. Fate was informing them that they were at a turning point.

That was because...the pair from thirty years ago couldn't express themselves outside of battle. Their egos had been too big, which prevented them from getting any closer.

Or maybe that would have been solved with time to close their emotional distance.

But for Iska and Alice...

"Do you like pasta?"

"Iska, why do you like this painter?"

"As your rival, I have a right to know everything about you!"

They had *interacted* as humans, connected through their strengths and weaknesses and many other ways. Iska the Successor of the Black Steel and Alice the Ice Calamity Witch knew each other outside of the battlefield.

They'd met over and over, sometimes having missed connections, and they just couldn't get away, even if they tried.

They had an intimate bond—closer than anyone else—that had just barely stopped them from repeating the same mistake.

"...I'll apologize again. I'm sorry." Alice bit her lip as the ice melted away.

The wall dissolved, and their surroundings gradually returned to its original form.

CHAPTER 6

"I resented the Imperial forces who attacked the palace. I will never forgive the Saint Disciple who hurt the queen… But I won't take those feelings out on you."

"What about Sisbell?"

"I'll go after the House of Hydra. There might be proof… I want you to stay with the servants. The villa isn't safe, so keep away from it." Alice turned around to look behind her.

Sirens screamed from the streets through the night.

"I think the medics I requested are here… You must go. I don't want them to see us talking."

"Okay."

"…Iska."

"Hmm?"

"I'm glad I fell for you."

An inhibited smile spread across her lips…until Alice realized what she had said and gasped.

"I—I didn't mean it *like that*. I meant I'm glad things fell into place, so we can be rivals! Wh-why is your mouth hanging open? This is a critical time, you know!"

"And who's to blame?!"

He had *known* that wasn't what she meant, of course.

So why wouldn't his heart stop beating out of his chest?

They were supposed to be enemies. She was the witch who he'd been engaged in battle with until now…

—*Why do I feel so flustered?* It almost seemed like…actual magic had been cast on him, like he'd been bewitched.

"…I was just preparing myself because I thought it was another one of your traps."

"H-how rude. Why would *I* try to seduce *you*?! …Ugh! Just go. You narrowly escaped death, Iska. We'll settle things next time. You keep that in mind!"

Alice swished her dress around, turned her back to him, and started running, trying to hide her burning cheeks.

"Next time, huh?"

It would happen someday. Even if fate veered off course, their intention to settle things would never change. Iska and Alice felt the same way.

But it wouldn't happen right now.

Someday, a time would come for them to square off in their crusade.

Iska and Alice ran in their respective directions, knowing this feeling in their hearts.

Alice the Ice Calamity Witch headed to the palace where the flames of war still fanned.

Iska the Successor of the Black Steel sprinted to the countryside where his friends waited.

The two of them had no idea…that even stranger events were occurring as the battle at the palace carried on.

EPILOGUE 1

Darkest Before Dawn

At the same time as the rematch was unfolding between Iska the Successor of the Black Steel and Alice the Ice Calamity Witch...

"Don't you know? As the sun hides during the night, the moon keeps watch."

On the palace grounds...was a forest where gunfire shot by the Imperial forces did not reach. At the outskirts where the wind rustled, an old man in a wheelchair was illuminated by the moonlight.

His wheelchair creaked as he moved forward. "That's odd. Why would an imprisoned young lady get out of jail at the same time as an Imperial raid?"

"......"

"And why would you have the youngest princess on your back?"

The head of the Zoa, Growley. The strapping old man still sported the wound inflicted by the Saint Disciple Nameless on his shoulder before he had slipped out of the Moon Spire.

"Now, girl. I believe your name was Vichyssoise, was it?"

"Uh-oh. Busted."

The redhead in a coat stuck out her tongue like this was all a joke. Sisbell, the youngest princess of the House of Lou, was on her back, not showing any signs of waking up during their conversation, almost like she had been drugged.

"This wasn't part of the plan, Gramps. I thought you would be hyped about the Imperial raid."

"Sort of." Behind him, flames raged over the palace grounds.

There were signs of the Imperial troops withdrawing, but the man showed no interest.

"Vice is pursuing the Saint Disciple. As the head of household, I must act the part."

"Oh? So that means…"

"Did you think you could deceive my eyes?" he jeered hoarsely at her. There were probably five yards between them. He pointed at the redhead standing in front of him.

"Wasn't it your master who invited the Imperial army here?" he asked. "And you were responsible for the plot to kill the queen. The Hydra are moving below the surface. You wouldn't reveal yourselves, so I pretended not to notice. But now that you're trying to take the youngest princess, that's proof enough. I'm glad I followed the evening wind where it took me."

"Oh? You have a good head on your shoulders, Gramps, even in your old age."

Vichyssoise arched an eyebrow. She had been seen attempting to bring Sisbell to the Solar Spire. She had no way of talking herself out of the situation. If anything, she should have been nervous, at least.

"And does the House of Zoa know about this?"

"Needless conjecture only breeds chaos. I knew to wait until the time came."

"I see. Then you sniffed out this scheme on your own. I have to admit that this makes me think better of you, but the irony is that some things in the world are better left unknown."

"Like your mutant form?"

"......"

"I heard during the inquisition. You transformed into something inhuman when you attacked Sisbell in the eighth state."

At that moment, Vichyssoise was wearing a dark overcoat. Her bare feet that peeked out from under it were white and fascinating but clearly human.

The old man still had no idea what kind of monster she could become.

—*How about you show me?* Growley seemed to be challenging her.

"I think my age has made me skeptical. I can't believe things unless I have a gander at them with my own eyes, you see. Of course, I don't mind if you stay as you are, but don't think you can escape from me."

"Poor Grandpa." The witch snickered. "Do you *want* to retire? I hate to let you know that I'm busy delivering Sisbell. So I'll have to give you somebody else to fight."

"Hmm?"

"A witch even *more* terrifying than me."

Zoosh. A lukewarm gust of wind clung to his skin. Trees rustled. Miasma, an ominous zephyr—in the old tradition, it was believed to be noxious air, impure and poisonous. It sent goose bumps on Growley's skin.

"What?" He turned around.

"Ha-ha. Ha-ha." He heard a beguiling cackle come from someone—or several people—echoing past the trees.

"Bye, Gramps. See you never." Vichyssoise leaped, Sisbell still on her back.

She fled as though she weren't carrying another body on her. All the old man could do was curse her under his breath. He couldn't go after her. The whole place was blasted by the devilish wind, echoing with beguiling laughter. He couldn't help but shudder all over.

Something was coming.

Over seventy, the purebred felt a strange threat like nothing he had ever experienced before.

"Unearthly presence—name yourself!"

He sensed something leap. From behind him? He forced his wheelchair to turn and looked above. The moonlight shining down on him had been blocked.

So was the thing above him?

He looked up. It was floating in the air, as if to block the moon.

Conformism: Divine Mutant Star, ■lle ■ ■ ■ ■ (Code name: Test Subject E).

She wore a jet-black dress. Raven-black astral light stretched out in the sky, blocking the moonlight. He looked at her dreadfully bewitching figure but couldn't make out who she was. That was because her skin was jet-black, as though she had been blotted out by shadow. Only her eyes were twinkling like stars. All Growley could do was hold his breath as he looked up at her, a monster that surpassed human knowledge.

"...Are you...a witch?"

He didn't mean an astral mage but the malice that brought calamity to the world.

Yes. The youngest princess, Sisbell, had seen this in the past, and after that, she had lost the ability to take a step out of her room due to fear. This unknown monster was...

"Oh, this is unfortunate. It seems Voice still won't behave."

EPILOGUE I

"...What?"

"I'm far from stellar perfection. I'm not used to this astral power."

Her voice was doubled up. The feminine voice that captivated those who heard it was layered with the voice of an immeasurable monster, creating a perplexing reverberation.

"Hark, the glad sound."

The dark witch floated in the air, blocking the moon and spreading both her arms. She sounded like the singer of an opera hall.

"Hear the requiem of the stars."

Several hours later, the astral corps who passed only managed to recover Growley's wheelchair.

Dawn broke. All the retainers and soldiers shivered upon sight of the bulletin plastered on the palace.

One person was out of commission:

—Queen Mirabella Lou Nebulis IIX: Alive.

Three were missing:

—House of Lou, Eldest Princess Elletear: Captured by Imperial army.

—House of Lou, Youngest Princess Sisbell: Captured by Imperial army at the villa.

—Head of the Zoa, Growley: MIA. Witnesses wanted.

EPILOGUE 2

*A Girl Offering Prayers
to Ten Billion Stars*

Her vision was white.

The floor, ceiling, and walls had been painted in sterile white. Even the bed on which she laid was white.

"...Where is this place...? Ouch."

As soon as she got up, she felt pain shooting through the back of her scalp. She hesitantly fingered the small lump on her head. Something had hit her, which must have caused her to lose consciousness.

"Iska?" Her weakened voice rang emptily in the room. "...Commander Mismis? Nene? Jhin?"

Where was the Imperial unit who had been protecting her?

She had been running for her life from Lord Talisman's private army in the villa. But she had no recollection of the events following that.

"Ngh. No!" The youngest princess gulped when she scanned the room again.

There were *no doors*. How had she gotten into this room? From some sort of astral power? Or was there a hidden door somewhere?

"......" Dread started to creep over Sisbell.

Iska and the rest of the Imperial unit weren't here. She had been tossed into this room alone, and there wasn't even a door to leave it.

There was one thing she could guess about the situation...

"...Have I...been kidnapped...?"

She tried to mentally retrace her steps. They had been facing against the Hydra, which meant this was probably the Solar Spire. It wouldn't be strange if they had a hidden room or two.

But what were they planning to do now that they had captured her? She would have exposed with Illumination that the House of Hydra had been trying to kill the queen. So she was a threat to them.

Was this an attempt to silence her? No. If that was the case, they wouldn't have shut her away into this hidden room. Was she a hostage to use against the Lou family? Or were they going to try winning her over and use her power for one of their schemes?

"This isn't funny. Who would obey them?!"

All her screams bounced off the walls. Even though she knew it was in vain, Sisbell continued, straining her voice. She did it to encourage herself, to keep herself from succumbing to the fear that was about to overtake her.

...I'm not going to lose. You have to be brave, Sisbell!

...This isn't a first for me, remember?

She had experienced something similar in the past. She remembered the fear that had crushed her after she had been caught and threatened with a gruesome death. What did she really have to fear? Compared to that, this was nothing.

"..." Sisbell placed her hand on her chest and steadied her heart.

Remember. Back then, someone had come to help her. There had been an eccentric Imperial soldier who *released* her from the Imperial prison.

EPILOGUE 2

* * *

"*Keep quiet. I'm gonna let you out right now.*"
"*Why are you...letting me escape...?*"

From that moment on, she believed—and continued to believe—that Unit 907 would never abandon her.

"...What good will it do to lose faith now?!"

She squeezed the hem of her sleeve, quivering. Her lips trembled.

"Astral powers that guide this planet, I beg of you."

She prayed to the stars.

If prayers held power, she would offer as many as she needed.

"Please deliver my message to Unit 907...!"

Afterword

Do the fate of the stars want a farewell or...?

Thank you for picking up *Our Last Crusade or the Rise of a New World*, Volume 7.

We kicked off Chapter 1 by diving straight into an all-consuming war. How did you like it?

The theme of this volume was generational changes. As shots are fired between the Empire and the Sovereignty, one blade looms near the queen... The Nebulis Sovereignty is in total upheaval. And it feels like its relationship with the Empire is about to face a dramatic change.

The most important question is...how will the new generation—Iska and Alice—face the fate shared by the transcendental sorcerer and the queen from the old era...? I was hoping to deliver this plot to you.

Intermission time. I want to touch on something before I talk about Volume 7 in depth.

AFTERWORD

...How do I go about saying this?

......

I'm so sorry about the delay!

I was battling some writer's block when thinking up plot developments for this series, but I think I caused readers some unnecessary worry, especially with rumors going around that I got sick. I apologize for making you wait.

I'm alive and well!

In fact, I'm so well that I've finished most of the manuscript for Volume 8. I know I made you wait for Volume 7, but I'm hoping that I'll have enough good news to make up for it.

Aaaand getting back to the topic at hand.

This volume wasn't just focused on the story between Alice and Iska or the queen and the transcendental sorcerer. A big part of the plot was the purebreds versus the Saint Disciples. I'm hoping I made up for some of the delays by presenting you with a content-rich volume.

I'm attached to some specific scenes.

The face-off between Kissing and Mei was almost roguish yet life-threatening, giving it a certain charm.

The head of household, Zoa, Growley, and Nameless unintentionally touch upon the theme of generational changes, which is fitting for experienced veterans.

Then there's the difference in what justice means for the Nebulis Sovereignty and Empire.

I put the spotlight on the Sovereignty, since they're the ones being attacked in this volume, though Mei and Nameless touch on the Empire's unnegotiable objectives in their conversation. This has been in progress for a while.

AFTERWORD

To think the fate of the two supernations will come together through the love between Alice and Iska. I hope you picked up on these hints in Volume 7.

Volume 8 is in the works. I think it'll come out in winter.

We're chugging toward the final stage of the war in the Sovereignty. I plan on sprinkling in more romantic elements into the story and more battles. I hope you're looking forward to it!

▼ Addendum

I have so many stories I want to write about the pair from the older generation (Mira and Salinger). I would love to write a side story about them sometime!

Anyway, that's enough reminiscing for now. I'm excited to make several announcements.

There is going to be a Fantasia Bunko Appreciation Festival in October in Akihabara, Tokyo. I will be there signing autographs.

▼ Fantasia Bunko Appreciation Festival 2019 Autograph Event
Sunday, October 20

Location: Belle Salle Akihabara. (Within walking distance from Akihabara Station.)

The ticket raffle will be held at Melonbooks in Akihabara!

By the time this book is published, you should be able to find more information on Fantasia Bunko's Twitter account, as well as on mine. I've been invited to autographing events in the past, but this is my first time participating in one sponsored by Fantasia. I'm really looking forward to it.

But wait—there's more!

Since this will be at the Fantasia Bunko Appreciation Festival, there will apparently be series merch on sale and on display. I hope you'll stop by for a good time!

AFTERWORD

*　*　*

▼ Announcement about *Our Last Crusade or the Rise of a New World*'s manga

Illustrated by okama, the manga is currently being serialized in the magazine *Young Animal*. Volume 2 was recently published, and it details the climax of Volume 1 of the light novel. The serialized chapters are currently covering content from Volume 3 of the light novels.

I would be so happy if you enjoy it as a companion to the novels.

And one more announcement: I'd like to introduce another story that I'm writing as I publish this series.

▼ MF Bunko J

Why Does No One Remember My World?

Volume 7 is out. I'm currently working on Volume 8.

Both the novels and manga are receiving great reception. I had an autographing event for this series in July, and I'm grateful to all the people who came!

And finally, I would like to write some words of gratitude.

To the illustrator, Ao Nekonabe.

Thank you so much for the gorgeous cover illustration and featuring Kissing with her cuteness boosted to 120 percent. The oodles of thorns are beautiful and terrifying, and this illustration made me want to involve Kissing in more of the plot.

To my editor, Y.

Thank you for reading through my work—long and short—and going above and beyond to organize events for *Our Last Crusade or the Rise of a New World*. You've been so thoughtful about every little detail, and you're just so considerate. I'm so glad to be in your care.

AFTERWORD

I know we're about to kick it into high gear, so I am counting on you for your help in the future!

Finally, I'd like to thank everyone who picked up this volume.

This is the tale of Iska the swordsman and Alice the witch princess.

As both the Empire and the Nebulis Sovereignty usher in a new age, the fate of the stars will involve the two—whether they like it or not.

I hope you expect great things from Volume 8, which is going to shake up their world.

I hope that we'll meet in *Our Last Crusade or the Rise of a New World*, Volume 8, which is slated for winter. And again, I hope you'll come to the 2019 Fantasia Bunko Appreciation Festival if you can.

(I think there will be lots to see…!)

On an afternoon in midsummer,

Kei Sazane

By the way, my personal account is *https://twitter.com/sazanek*.

I'll post the latest announcements there. I hope you'll check it out every once in a while!

Announcement: VOLUME 8

Bring on the applause and cheers! Bring on your deep-seated resentment— all to topple the Empire!

The queen of Nebulis has fallen, shaking up the Sovereign government. The three bloodlines begin to work toward their own goals, raging against the Empire. To recover Sisbell, Iska is desperately trying to negotiate with Alice on one condition. Now knowing each other's objectives, Alice is called to make a choice…

Reaching the eighth act of the tale, a new bloodline of the Founder stirs with activity—as paradise begins to fall.

❖ The content of this book is subject to change without advance notice.

VOLUME 8
Coming soon

Our Last CRUSADE OR THE RISE OF A New World

KIMI TO BOKU NO SAIGO NO SENJO,
ARUI WA SEKAI GA HAJIMARU SEISEN
©okama 2019 / HAKUSENSHA, Inc.
©2018 Kei Sazane · Ao Nekonabe / KADOKAWA
THE WAR ENDS THE WORLD / RAISES THE WORLD
©Kei Sazane, Ao Nekonabe 2017
/ KADOKAWA CORPORATION

LIGHT NOVEL

MANGA

LOVE IS A BATTLEFIELD

When a princess and a knight from rival nations fall in love, will they find a way to end a war or remain star-crossed lovers forever...?

AVAILABLE NOW WHEREVER BOOKS ARE SOLD!

For more information visit www.yenpress.com

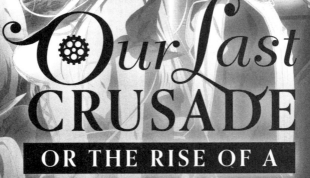